SABINE

By the same author:

Circle of Doom

SABINE

Tim Kennemore

Andersen Press • London

First published in 2003 by
Andersen Press Limited,
20 Vauxhall Bridge Road, London SW1V 2SA
www.andersenpress.co.uk

British Library Cataloguing in Publication Data available
ISBN 1 84270 291 2

Typeset by FiSH Books, London WC1
Printed and bound in Great Britain by
Mackays of Chatham Ltd., Chatham, Kent

For Tom and Ruth

1

'Get out the way, Squash, you moron!'

'Mind the baby!'

'Wanna get squashed, Squash? Wanna get *squished*?'

'Run for your life, Squash. Run!'

Josh ducked his head and ran, swerving from side to side to keep out of the way of the boys thundering up and down the football pitch, and dodging thc ball that flew through the air – always, it seemed, in his direction. Josh knew from experience how hard that ball was if it hit you, and it felt twice as hard if you weren't expecting it.

He made it to the other side, where he had his own quiet place, sitting on a low wall that ran along the side of Year 3's classroom. Unfortunately Josh wasn't in Year 3, and so, every single day, he had to suffer the ordeal of crossing the football pitch to get here. Four times. At break and at lunch; there and back again.

Break was the worst time of the day to be alone. Lessons had a purpose, and even at lunchtime there was eating to be done. But the only reason for break was for people to play with their friends, and there was no way that Josh could pretend even to himself that he had one any more. His only friend had gone.

He tore open his crisps and began to crunch his way through them. *Claudio*, he thought, and then he tried to think of something else, because every time Claudio came into his mind – which was often – it made him sad, and sometimes it almost made him cry. Claudio had been his friend for three wonderful years, ever since he'd arrived from Italy with his parents and his sister. Josh hadn't really understood that they wouldn't be staying for ever.

'Two years still we're going to be here,' Claudio had said, which sounded like eternity, and then, 'We go back the end of next year', which sounded the same. Even 'We go back after Christmas' never sounded real. Surely nothing so awful could happen? Why would it?

And then Christmas came round, and the last day of term, which should have been fun with a party and games, was Claudio's last day, and Josh sat transfixed in a fog of misery and gloom. Even then he thought they might change their minds during the holidays. It was only when he came back for the first day of the Easter term, and Claudio really wasn't there, not there and *not going to be there ever again*, that it finally sank in. And Josh's whole world collapsed around him.

You needed to be part of a gang to get by if you were a boy. Claudio had always laughed at the gangs, especially at Shane Walters and his gang who were the biggest and the worst, and somehow Claudio always got away with it. He was small but there was something tough about him. People didn't mess with Claudio. He could curse in fluent Italian, which made them nervous. But mostly he just laughed. He didn't take them seriously at all.

Josh would have loved to be able not to take Shane Walters seriously but he had no idea how it was done. Josh was small and there was *nothing* tough about him. And his hair was too long. His mother liked it that way.

She liked to rumple his hair. She thought he looked adorable. Grown-ups generally thought he was cute. Even girls thought he looked cute, which was the most disastrous thing of all.

All the boys hated his guts.

The bell sounded for the end of break. Josh munched up the loose broken bits at the bottom of his crisp bag, scrunched it up and summoned his courage for the return journey across the football pitch.

The ball was down the far end. If he made a run for it now, he might get to the other side while all the action was still a long way away from him.

He set off, his head down, looking at the ground, almost as if this might protect him. *If you can't see them they can't see you.* He tried everything he knew to make himself invisible. The football game was breaking up, the boys collecting their jumpers, racing and charging, bumping and bouncing. He was almost safe.

And then *thwack!* a sudden huge crushing blow on the side of his head. Because he hadn't been looking up he hadn't known it was coming. The shock made him stumble and brought tears stinging to his eyes.

The yells of the boys fell silent. There was a dark uncomfortable unease. Even through the thudding pain Josh could sense that they were circling around him at a distance, curious to know if he was hurt and at the same time anxious not to get involved.

'You all right?' The voice spoke from a few yards away. Shane Walters.

'I'm OK,' Josh said, furiously wiping the tears from

his eyes. He didn't look round. He set off walking towards the school building, towards the classroom. He just wanted to get away. But his voice had told Shane Walters all he needed to know.

'Why you crying then? Crybaby! Baby!' The tension behind him dissolved into relief. He hadn't been hurt, and so nobody was going to get into trouble. 'Squash baby dumpling, baby got a thumping!' 'Awwwwwww!' 'Leeeckle baby!'

The tears of shock, which would have disappeared all by themselves in a few moments, were turning into proper tears of shame. Josh ran into the toilets and hid, squeezing his eyes dry with toilet paper until he felt quite sure he wouldn't cry any more. He could see in the mirror that his face told the whole story. His eyes were red and his cheeks smudged where the tears had run into some dirt he hadn't known was there. He washed his face one last time and checked it again.

He still didn't look right. He would have given everything he had in the world to be able to go home. Home was only five minutes' walk away. But his mum would be there with Luke, and his mum wasn't the same person she'd been a few months ago, before there was Luke. She wouldn't have time for him and his problems. She'd be all exhausted from looking after Luke, and she would send Josh straight back to school, and he'd arrive in the middle of the lesson and everyone would look at him, and all the boys would nudge and laugh and whisper, 'Gosh it's Squash! Gosh! Did the baby go home for its bottle? Did Squash want its baby nosh?'

There was nothing for it but to go to the classroom and carry on.

Josh slipped around the door and slid into his seat. Thank goodness his seat was right at the back of the room, because the door was at the back too, and so nobody really noticed him. Shane Walters and his gang had moved on to the next thing already; someone had given Jake O'Donnell a dead leg and Josh was, for the moment at least, forgotten.

Josh sat behind two girls called Carrie Lindwell and Bethany Marks. They were always turning round to talk to him, and he *thought* they liked him, but with girls it was never possible to be sure. Sometimes he thought they were teasing him. Sometimes he thought that if he wasn't very careful they might reach over and rumple his hair. Girls were tricky.

Carrie turned round now, and with that radar all girls seemed to have she knew straightaway that something was wrong.

'Ooh, Josh. What's the matter?'

'Nothing,' said Josh, but Bethany's head had snapped round at the first inkling of drama, and Bethany was if anything even sharper than Carrie.

'You look like you've been crying,' she said. Both their faces were crumpled into expressions of concern. It left Josh feeling confused. It was nice to think that somebody cared about him, but at the same time he wished they wouldn't. It was all too easy to start crying again when people were nice to you and made a fuss. It was better to think about something else altogether, until you were past the danger point.

‘I’m OK,’ he said. ‘Just got hit in the head by a football by accident. It stings a bit, that’s all.’

‘Oooooh!’ Purrs of sympathy from the girls. ‘You poor thing!’ said Carrie. Josh winced. He knew full well that it hadn’t been an accident at all. The football game had finished. Shane Walters had belted the ball directly at Josh as hard as he could, for no other reason than that Josh was there and Shane hated him.

Best not to think about that. He fought to find something safe to fill up his mind, and soon fell back on an old trick, saying the alphabet backwards in his head. This was too difficult to do without a lot of thought, which meant it was usually good enough to take his mind off anything nasty.

Bethany and Carrie had swivelled back round to face the front and were whispering together. Josh had only got to K in the alphabet backwards but he felt it was probably safe to stop. He had actually got to K really quickly. Maybe he was starting to *learn* the alphabet backwards, which was terrible because if it became easy it wouldn’t work any more for taking his mind off things, and he would have to find something different.

He lifted his schoolbag onto the seat next to him and got out his reading book for the next lesson. He tried always to keep something on the chair in case anyone should take it into their head to sit next to him. That seat had been Claudio’s, and nobody was going to take Claudio’s place if Josh had anything to do with it. A new boy had arrived in their class after Christmas, and Josh had seen Miss Hollis eyeing up Claudio’s old seat and making her plans. How convenient, she would be thinking. Josh is all on his own now. He can look after the new boy. He'll probably be glad of the company.

Josh was having none of it. He spread all his possessions out on Claudio's old desk and chair, covering every inch of the surface, folded his arms and glowered. The new boy was called William Beresford. He was tall and bone-thin, with that white-blond hair that you sometimes see on little kids, but which most people of William's age have grown out of. He wore thin-rimmed glasses, he looked spotlessly clean and he couldn't be more different from Claudio if he tried.

Miss Hollis got the message, and gave William a seat somewhere else, leaving Josh alone. He wasn't sure if William Beresford had noticed all this. He didn't honestly care.

Bethany and Carrie stopped whispering and turned round again.

'Have you got a Technomon, Josh?' Bethany asked.

'A what?'

'Technomon. You *know*.'

'Is it collectable cards?' Josh was wary of collectable cards. They were brilliant when you started off, when nearly every packet you bought contained different cards, ones you didn't have. But then the duplicates began to arrive, and you had to spend more and more money just to keep going. It would be OK if you were in a gang and could swap them around, but Josh could do nothing but watch in despair as his duplicates mounted up. When he collected Pokémon cards he'd ended up with *fourteen* Bellsprouts. So he wasn't too keen on starting over with another kind. But:

'No, silly, it's on the Internet. You do have the Internet?'

Josh nodded. He was allowed to use the family computer quite a lot, especially since Luke had arrived.

Bethany and Carrie began to talk in this way they had, almost as if they were singing a duet. Both of them seemed to know when the other one would pause and they always had their next line ready. It was extraordinary. It was as if they were reading from a script.

'Well, what it is, you go to the website and join . . .'

'You don't have to pay or anything, it's all free . . .'

'And you choose an egg and it hatches into a pet . . .'

'And you have to feed and take care of it and it grows up.'

'Oh.' Josh had heard of this kind of thing before. It all sounded terribly girly.

'I've got a Luponio,' said Bethany. 'It's nearly six weeks old now. It's *adorable*.'

'I've got a Forkfoot,' said Carrie.

'Is this a girl thing?' asked Josh.

'No, silly. Everybody does it. My brother's got a Muckslime. It's absolutely disgusting.'

Josh knew Carrie Lindwell's brother. He was eight years old. He was young enough to get away with having a computer pet called a Muckslime without getting laughed at.

'Anyway,' said Bethany, 'why don't you have one of these Technomon mousemats? We won them in a painting competition.'

‘I really don’t think . . . ’ said Josh, but it was too late; the mousemat had already arrived on his desk. It was every bit as cute as he’d imagined. Bright cheerful colours, with sweet cartoony animals gambolling and frisking through the grass and leaping out of the river. The river flowed around a central flat-topped mountain, above which floated a halo of silvery stars. Still more of the sickeningly adorable pets – Technomon – were flying high in the sky.

Josh saw some boys looking his way, and stuffed the mousemat in his bag. ‘Thanks,’ he said. ‘But I . . . ’

But at that moment Miss Hollis swept in with a fluster of tapping heels and baggy cardigan, and Carrie and Bethany snapped around to face the front. Time for work.

2

At the end of school Josh went round to the Infants to collect his sister Molly. The timing of this was always tricky. He didn't want to get there too soon because of all the mothers milling around, who liked nothing better than to pounce on him. But he couldn't be too late and leave Molly waiting after everyone else had gone.

Today he almost got it right. Molly was standing in the doorway of her classroom, which led straight into the playground, and there was just one mother still lurking. Unfortunately she was one of the difficult ones. She was gushy and lipsticky and she wore long flowery dresses. Her daughter, Jessica something, was always perfectly clean and tidy, even at the end of school. There was something not quite right about that.

'Josh! Hello!' said Jessica's mother, homing in on him with relish.

Josh mumbled hello, trying not to sound encouraging.

'And how's the little one? How's your baby brother? And how's your poor mother?'

Josh had had months of this by now. 'They're all right,' he said, although he knew, and he knew Jessica's mother knew, that if they were really all right they'd *be* here, picking up Molly and Josh, with Luke dozing in a pushchair like all the other babies. All the mothers were desperate for information, and it was no use asking

Molly anything because Molly lived on another planet. So they all waited for Josh. At the start it had been 'Any news from the hospital, dear?' *every single day*. And the hospital wasn't something Josh wanted to talk to these women about. He didn't entirely understand what was happening there, and anyway he didn't see how it was anyone's business outside their family. But they didn't seem to understand that. The less he said, the more they asked. Dozens of times he'd felt like saying: 'How am I supposed to know this stuff? I'm not a doctor.' He supposed they were being kind but mostly it felt like they were poking their noses in.

Jessica's mother was one of the most persistent, and she kept trying a while longer, but after getting nothing more out of Josh than shrugs and mumbles, she gave up and left, with a final 'Please tell your mother I'm thinking of her! And please do let me know if there's anything I can do to help!' Her words sounded warm but her manner had cooled. Josh guessed that she was disappointed with him for being rude. In other circumstances she would most probably have said so.

He grabbed Molly, who was humming softly to herself and watching the sky.

'What's that woman's name?' he asked her, as they crossed the playground.

'What woman?'

'The one I was just talking to.'

'I don't know. I wasn't looking.'

Josh sighed. 'Jessica's mother.'

'*Oh*!'

There was a pause.

'So go on then.'

'Go on where?'

'What's her name?'

'I don't know,' said Molly.

It was like talking to an alien. Josh tried again.

'What's Jessica's surname?'

'Hallam,' said Molly, and then: 'Oh, yes! Her mother's called Patricia Hallam!' her voice sounding almost surprised, as if it were a tremendous coincidence that Jessica and her mother should share the same name.

Molly slipped her hand into his when they reached the road, although Bob the lollipop man was still there and it was perfectly safe. She always did this. It was another reason why Josh put off collecting her as long as possible after school had finished. By now there was hardly anybody around to see.

Molly was small, like Josh, and she too had long hair and was generally thought to be cute as a button, but when you were a girl these things all counted in your favour. Her hair was dark blonde, the colour of honey (Josh's hair was only a whisper darker but his was definitely light brown) and, unlike Jessica Hallam, by the end of school Molly was a mess. There was a smudge on her cheek, her socks had fallen down, one of her shoelaces had come loose and her hair was matted in scruffy knots. Come to think of it, she didn't look that much different at the *beginning* of school. Did anybody brush Molly's hair these days? Josh couldn't remember.

Molly hung onto his hand, although Josh was walking

as fast as he could and she had to do little skips every few steps to keep up. She kept up the usual flow of chatter. 'We had a story about a pig that joined the circus, and we did our Easter baskets. I'm going to give my Easter basket to Mummy. Tomorrow we're going to paint the eggs. Aaron Fraser was sick all over the floor after lunch. You could see the carrots in the sick. It was *gross*.'

'That's nice,' said Josh, scarcely listening. 'Molly, pay attention while we cross the road.' There was just this one more road that had to be crossed between school and home. Sometimes Josh half wished they lived further away, and then his mum would *have* to come and fetch them and he wouldn't have to walk his baby sister to and from school every day. Next year he was changing schools but there was a whole summer to get through before then. And in any case Josh hated the thought of moving up to the new school. At his present school, even if he wasn't big he was one of the oldest. At the new school he'd be one of the youngest. Quite probably he would be the smallest person in the whole place. Perhaps his life was going to get even worse.

When they got home their mother was sitting in the kitchen, leaning forward with her arms slumped on the table. Luke, the baby, was in his carrycot. He was making little snuffly noises but he seemed to be about three-quarters asleep. Apart from the low humming of the refrigerator there was no other noise. The blinds were half drawn, casting shadow stripes across the table. It was a room that made you want to tiptoe and to whisper.

'How's he been today?' Josh said softly to his mother. 'Did he drink his milk up?' Please, oh please, let Luke have drunk his milk. The mood of the house depended on it. The entire Harper family were helpless, their peace, their life, sometimes it seemed their entire future, totally in the hands of this tiny creature.

Josh's mother sat halfway up in the chair. 'He took most of his morning feed. And then he slept for two whole hours.'

'Wow, that's good.' Luke hardly ever slept for such a long time. His parents, and especially his mother, were often up with him the whole night through.

'But he's scarcely touched his afternoon feed.' His mother waved wearily at a bottle sitting by the microwave. 'He just took one and a half ounces and then he was sick.'

'Oh.' The amount remaining in the bottle looked so little. Barely a mouthful. But every drop was vital because Luke was still so small. If he lost any weight, they'd take him back into hospital.

Josh wasn't sure that this wouldn't be the best thing. Luke was so very frail and tiny. In hospital at least he would be safe. They could keep a proper eye on him, and if he didn't take his milk they could put a tube back in and feed him that way. And there would be lots of nurses around to help take care of him, and his mother wouldn't be so exhausted all the time. But he knew his mother didn't feel that way. She had wanted quite desperately to bring Luke home, and now she had him here her greatest fear was that he would have to go back.

Luke had been born three months early, changing the

Harper family forever. At first the doctors hadn't even been sure if he was strong enough to live. He had arrived so soon, before his lungs were properly grown. Josh's father had explained this to him in the evenings, after Molly was in bed. His mother was at the hospital with Luke. She even slept there, every night until Luke came home.

Josh had ached for that day to come, because it meant that at last he'd get his mother back. But now he was beginning to see that that wasn't necessarily true. Her actual physical body might be here but her mind and her thoughts and her heart were somewhere else.

'There was this woman at school,' he said – too loudly, for Luke gave a little shudder and a cry, and time stood still for half a minute while he hovered between wakefulness and sleep. The disturbance hung over the carrycot like a thundery black cloud. But then, with a tiny cough, he settled down again, the cloud broke up and the room returned to normal.

His mother, who hadn't breathed since the cry, let out a long deep sigh.

'Sorry,' Josh said in a half whisper. 'Anyway, what I was going to say. There was this woman, she's called Patricia Hallam? She said to give you her best wishes and to let her know if there's anything she can do. To help out. Or anything.' However little Josh liked Patricia Hallam – which was *very* little – he thought it was time his mother began to reconnect to the outside world. He was less proud of his other reason for passing the message on, which was that if people were able to get information directly from his mother they would surely leave him alone.

But: 'That's kind,' she said, and Josh knew she wouldn't give it another thought.

'Well, OK. Is there anything you'd like me to do?'

'I don't think so. Do we still have any of those chicken pieces left in the freezer?'

'Enough for two more meals.'

'And chips?'

'Just about enough for one meal but not for big helpings.'

'Well, that'll do for tea then. I think I might...'

Her head was starting to nod. Josh tiptoed out of the room. Once upon a time she'd have wanted to know all about his day, but things were different now. Molly had accepted how the world had changed. Molly had a knack for accepting, and just getting on with things. She'd gone straight up to her room, where she would be playing one of her complicated pretend games with dolls and stick people, or the chocolate seahorse family, or the Lego Block Monsters, or Loopy Rose the space cucumber and her one-legged moonfriend Stumpy John of Bald.

It would be another two hours till his father came home. Even though the rest of his family were here in the house with him, Josh felt very much alone. There was so little time for his mother to do things with him now, and this was one of those rare opportunities, and she preferred to doze. He knew it was because she wasn't able to sleep at night, and he tried very hard not to mind, but somehow it left an empty feeling right at the centre of him. Because however tired she was, she would always wake up for Luke. Once perhaps she had cared about Josh that much, although he had been born at the right time and had never been ill at all ever, other than runny noses and coughs and things everybody got.

He went into the computer room and began to click around idly with the mouse. There were a few games installed on the machine that he quite liked to play for fifteen or twenty minutes, but he had two whole hours to kill and in any case he didn't feel like any of them. What he needed was something different, something absorbing that would fill up his mind and push all his worries out of the way. Maybe at the weekend his father would buy him a new game. Josh felt the stirrings of hope. He and his father and Molly would probably be going into town for a few hours to give his mother a rest, and that would be the perfect opportunity. He'd overheard some boys in his class talking about a game called *Stargate Infinity*, which had sounded brilliant. If Josh could get *Stargate Infinity* and really work at it for a couple of weeks he might be able to catch up with the others, or even get ahead, and he could talk about it with them at break.

This was an excellent plan but it had a lot of *ifs* in it, and in any case it wasn't the slightest help to him right now.

Then he remembered the mousemat.

Technomon. Cutely adorable dipsy little virtual cartoon pets.

It wasn't his kind of thing at all. He was quite sure of that.

But what harm could it do to have a look? His parents had always told him he was too inclined to dismiss things without giving them a proper chance. You miss out that way, they told him. Sometimes you never even try something that you would actually really like, if you were only prepared to give it a go.

But I *know* what I like, Josh always said. It's a waste of energy to spend it trying things out when you already know you won't like them.

And his parents had shrugged and sighed and told him he was making a big mistake. It had happened over and over. It happened with judo, with summer activity week, with learning the violin, with at least a dozen books people had bought him but which Josh knew he would hate just from reading the back cover. It had happened with boys they'd wanted to invite over for Josh to meet, and with countless kinds of food including any sort of fish whatever.

And it would probably have happened with Technomon, if he hadn't been quite so lonely and desperate for something to do.

He would just quickly check out the website.

Nobody need ever know. Nobody *would* ever know.

He reached into his bag and pulled out the mousemat.

3

Welcome to Technopolis!
The greatest virtual pet centre on the Internet!
Raise your own Technomon!
More than six million owners already!

The rainbow letters rippled across the screen in a dazzling display of colour. You almost needed sunglasses just to look at it.

There were at least a dozen different buttons on this first page, all leading off to other parts of the site. Technopolis was *huge*. Josh didn't know where to start. **Your Pet**, **Your Account**, **Shopping Mall**, **Games Centre**, **Message Boards**, **World Map**, **Newsroom**, **Help** . . .

Josh clicked on **Help**, and another screen displayed, with a new selection of buttons, one of which said **Newbie Guide**.

This seemed like the place to start.

Josh read that the first thing he needed to do was to set up an account. Then he could set about getting a pet right away. He could either adopt an existing Technomon or start from scratch with an egg. If he chose to hatch an egg, he would be given a gift of 500 Technickels to spend on its upkeep. If he went for adoption, he would get 1000 Technickels, as a reward for taking on someone else's abandoned pet.

Josh created an account with the player name *Shadow Demon* and the password *laserbeam*. Then he decided to check out the Adoption Centre, at the top of Mount Caranthus. There were hundreds of Technomon up for adoption, but all of them were Level 1 – the very lowest level, and none of them had learned any skills or acquired any talents at all.

The Adoption Guide explained why this should be.

Pets are put up for adoption when they are unwanted for some reason, or if their owners can no longer care for them. Higher level pets are offered for adoption much more rarely, and when they appear are snapped up immediately. You would need tremendous good luck to find one.

Josh doubted that he would have that kind of luck. Why were so many Technomon abandoned by their owners while they were still so young? Most of the pets in the Adoption Centre were less than a day old. Perhaps the owners didn't like the look of them once they'd hatched, and preferred to try again. Maybe some baby Technomon were really ugly, or whiny, or too dumb to learn. You couldn't really blame people for dumping them. Life was cruel that way. Even Technolife.

But if Josh was going to start off with a baby, he wanted one he'd hatched himself from an egg, not somebody else's reject. Probably everyone felt the same. He'd be 500 Technickels worse off, but there were bound to be ways of raising more.

He clicked on **Your Pet** and then on **Choose an Egg**

feeling a little buzz of excitement. Choosing was always fun. *Everyone* loved to choose. But before he could get to the eggs there was a page to read about the responsibilities involved in taking on a pet.

These were considerable. Josh would have to feed it, play with it, teach it and train it. He would have to make sure it got sufficient exercise, and supervise its health. The personality his Technomon would develop depended entirely on Josh, and on the upbringing he gave it.

A *lot* of responsibilities. For a moment Josh hesitated. Was this really something he wanted to do? It seemed like a great deal of work, and he had enough problems in his life already without suffering pangs of guilt because he'd been neglecting his virtual pet.

He shook his head. No need to take this so seriously. It was just a game. If he got bored he could just put the pet up for adoption, like everyone else did. He made a silent promise that however boring the game, however unsuitable the pet, he wouldn't abandon it until it was at least at Level Two and had learned some skills. Then he could be sure someone else would take it on.

With that settled in his mind, he clicked on **Show Me My Eggs**, and a new screen loaded. Five eggs were sitting in a nest of straw: one pale green, one blue with purple speckles, one blue with green speckles, one pinky-red and one mauve. The eggs were numbered one to five.

Move your mouse over an egg to see the silhouette of the Technomon growing inside. Click on the silhouette to learn about that Technomon. To choose an egg, click on its number. You will be asked to confirm your choice. And that's it! The start of your incredible adventure with your very own pet!

The Technomon in the eggs were:

1. Springray. A bouncy little fish with a tightly coiled body. Springray swim in large shoals, a magnificent sight at night when they all glow in different colours. Most commonly found in the warm waters of the Luettan Sea, off the south-east coast of Technopolis. Strength: 2. Speed: 7. Intelligence: 6. Sociability: 9.

2. Flagondra. This friendly little dragon loves to play. But beware! Mistreat it, or take advantage of its good nature, and you will feel the power of its flaming breath. Herds of Flagondra inhabit the Scorched Forest north of the Marmolean Plain, most of which they have, over the years, burned down. Strength: 6. Speed: 3. Intelligence: 6. Sociability: 10.

3. Luponio. Half wolf, half horse, the Luponio is the most unpredictable of all Technomon, since it combines the characteristics of both. It can be as cunning as a wolf, or as steadfast and loyal as a horse. These pets must be carefully reared if their finer nature is to triumph. Luponio can be found all over Technopolis, alone or in very small groups. Strength: 7. Speed: 8. Intelligence: 6. Sociability: 3.

4. Glostrich. A tall, long-legged bird with a magnificent coat of shiny feathers tipped with jewels, the Glostrich takes its looks seriously and can spend as many as four hours a day grooming itself. The nesting grounds of the Glostrich are in the dry grasslands of the south west. This bird shuns the company of other Glostrich, preferring to display its

gaudy finery without competition.
Strength: 5. Speed: 8. Intelligence: 7. Sociability: 2.

5. Tedrapod. Since first domesticated in the early years of Technopolis, Tedrapod have remained one of the most popular kinds of pet. Strong and powerful, they make excellent guards, while their lovable tumbling tricks are a source of constant entertainment. The natural habitat of the Tedrapod is the Sable Forest, near the foothills of Mount Caranthus.
Strength: 9. Speed: 3. Intelligence: 5. Sociability: 7.

Well. This decision wasn't going to be difficult. No way in the world was Josh having a fish for a pet. He *hated* fish. And the bird, the Glostrich, sounded like a total pain. He couldn't believe anyone would pick it.

The Luponio sounded interesting, but Carrie Lindwell or Bethany Marks had one (he couldn't remember which), and this was reason enough to avoid it.

And he wouldn't be seen dead owning a pet which, let's face it, was some kind of overgrown *teddy bear*.

Which left the dragon. The Flagondra. He liked the idea of a Flagondra. Dragons were cool. These Flagondra dragons sounded a bit too cute and friendly to be properly cool, but perhaps Josh could train it up to be fearsome, and go round flaming other Technomon, like those stupid Glostrich for example.

He took a deep breath, and clicked on egg number 2. Blue with purple speckles. It was ridiculous, but he actually felt quite a thrill. His own baby dragon was about to hatch before his very eyes.

Except that that wasn't what happened at all.

This was what happened: a message appeared on the screen saying:

Congratulations! You have just chosen your first Technomon!

Your egg will hatch some time in the next two days. While you're waiting, take the opportunity to explore Technopolis, visit the shops and try out the games – and get yourself prepared for your new arrival! See our Guide to Newborns *for our expert advice.*

Good luck!

Josh stared at the screen in disbelief. Two days? What was all that about? He wanted his egg now, not in two days' time! What was he supposed to do for two days? Buy bumper-sized packs of Technappies? Decorate the nursery with scorchproof paint? Mix up a dozen bottles of sterilised dragonmilk? He thumped the mouse down on the mousemat in a flash of frustrated temper. Technomon were rubbish. Even their mousemat was rubbish; the mouse scratched across the surface instead of sliding smoothly. He put the old mousemat back, and threw the Technomonstrosity across the desk. It bounced off the speaker and fell to the floor.

He was just wondering what to do next to fill the time till their father got home when, to his amazement, he heard the sound of a key in the front door. Dad back already? Had Josh really spent two whole hours lost in Technopolis? Surely that wasn't possible?

But it was true. Molly had heard the noise too and came

tumbling down the stairs. Josh ran out and collided with her in the hall. Their father picked them up, shook them down – no damage – and swung Molly up into a hug.

'Daddy! Hello! I'm making an Easter basket for Easter, and Loopy Rose had to go to the space doctor for her wobbles!'

'No! Was it serious?'

'Daddy! She only nearly died!'

'Goodness!' He looked worried. 'And hi there, Joshsky. What's been the story of your day? Nothing as serious as spacewobbles, I hope?'

But before Josh could say a word there came a high, piercing screech from the kitchen, the door opened and their mother looked round it, rubbing her eyes. She looked grumpy and not one bit pleased to see any of them.

'Can't you keep quiet? Now you've woken Luke up!'

'Linda, they have to be allowed to live in their own home,' their father said gently. He put an arm round their mother and led her back into the kitchen. Luke was screaming at full blast now. His father picked him up, took the barely-touched bottle in the other hand and began to feed him. Luke fell silent, drinking.

'You haven't warmed the milk,' said Mum. 'He won't drink it.'

'But he *is* drinking it, look.' And all of a sudden the atmosphere lightened. Luke was feeding. They could all breathe more easily.

Molly and Josh slipped into the kitchen. Josh noticed that they were both tiptoeing, even though there wasn't the slightest need. *They have to be allowed to live in their own house*, he thought, remembering his father's words. Was Luke's battle for survival sucking the life out of everyone else? It was a relief that Dad had noticed the possibility and wasn't going to let it happen.

Josh and his father organised tea together. It was the third time that week they'd had chicken and chips.

'We need more food,' his father said. 'More variety. We need to stock up the freezer.'

'We need more chips urgently,' said Josh.

'We can't live on chips,' said Dad.

Josh wouldn't have minded living on chips. 'We haven't got any breakfast cereal at all,' he said. 'And that banana Molly had this morning was the last fresh fruit.'

'I'm finishing work early tomorrow,' their father said. 'I'll go to the supermarket on the way home and do an enormous shop. How about that, Lin?'

'But you don't know what we need,' their mother said.

'I know what we need,' Josh said. 'I'll come with you, Dad.'

'Me too!' said Molly. 'Please?'

Their father looked unsure. 'I was going straight from work . . . '

'But you can just pick us up from school on the way!'

'We'll help you put all the bags in the car and get them out again!' said Molly.

Josh hoped it didn't sound too obvious that they were both absolutely desperate to go out with Dad rather than coming back home. He didn't want to hurt his mother's feelings. Molly was doing well to make it sound as if they were just very keen to help.

'I really do know all the stuff we need,' he said. 'And I know which aisles in the supermarket they keep it in! You'd get lost all by yourself. I'll save you so much time you'll end up being quicker if you come and fetch us. You just wait and see.'

Molly was nodding eagerly, and their father smiled and said all right, now he came to think of it he could use a couple of extra pairs of hands to help out. Molly bounced up and down and gave a little cheer. Josh sneaked a worried glance at his mother to see if she did look at all hurt, but she was watching Luke and didn't appear to have heard a single word.

4

Next morning there was no breakfast food of any kind to be found. Every last flake and crisp and cluster of cereal was gone. Josh went to fetch some bread to put in the toaster and found it all spotted with blue mould, so that was no good either.

'What's that you're making?' asked his father, sitting at the table gently rocking Luke on his lap. Mum was still in bed, grabbing an extra half-hour's sleep.

'Pop tarts.'

'For breakfast?'

'There's nothing else here.'

'Oh.' Brief silence. 'What flavour?'

'Chocolate,' said Josh. He knew his mother would never have allowed chocolate pop tarts for breakfast, but all the rules had changed now.

Dad shook his head ruefully. He wasn't good at early mornings and was never properly awake until he'd been up and about for an hour or two, and drunk quite a lot of coffee. 'Ah well. Supermarket today.'

'Shall I cook one for you? We've got enough.'

'I think,' said his father, 'that given a choice between eating a chocolate pop tart for breakfast and being fried to death in an electric chair, my answer would probably be "Plug me in".'

'I'll take that as a no,' said Josh. The toaster went

ping; he took his pop tart out and set another one going for Molly.

'I can't believe you're really going to eat that,' his father said, running his hand through his hair with a mystified expression as Josh sat down on the opposite side of the table. He propped Luke up to give him a better view. 'Look, Luke. See what terrible, terrible taste your brother has. Resolve to grow up different.' Luke's eyes were only half open but even so he seemed the more awake of the two of them. Josh waved at him but Luke didn't react. Josh was never sure if he could even see him.

Molly stumbled in, bleary and sleepy eyed and with her cardigan buttoned up all wrong. Her hair looked as if she'd been pulled backwards through a hedge.

'Dad,' said Josh. 'I don't think anybody's been brushing Molly's hair in the mornings.'

'Mmmm,' said their father, forcing his eyes fully open and taking in the sight of Molly. 'Oh, goodness.'

'Did anyone brush *your* hair?' Molly asked Josh.

'I can do mine with my fingers,' Josh said, demonstrating.

Molly tried to comb her hair through with her fingers, but immediately came up against a huge tangled knot.

'Molly,' said their father. 'Do you know where there's a hairbrush?'

'I've got a sparkly brush!' said Molly. 'I think I saw it last week somewhere. I'll go and look.'

'Now she's gone off without eating her breakfast,' Josh said fretfully. It was tough work, getting Molly to school on time both fed *and* tidy.

'From a nutritional point of view that's probably a blessing,' his father said. 'Josh, I'm going to make myself another coffee before I doze off. Can you take Luke or shall I fetch his carrycot down?'

'I'll take him,' Josh said, although he never felt entirely comfortable holding Luke. It was altogether too much responsibility. His father lowered the little bundle gently into his arms. It was impossible that anything so important could weigh so little. 'Hello, Goliath,' he said. He didn't expect Luke to get the joke, but the baby wouldn't even catch his eye, and began to make a faint grizzling noise. Josh picked up an unfinished bottle from the table – there was *always* an unfinished bottle somewhere near Luke – and eased the teat into his mouth, but after one hesitant suck the baby lost interest, and his body stiffened the way it did when he was unhappy about something. Josh hastily withdrew the bottle. I'm sorry, Luke, he said silently, in his head. I was trying to make you happy. I don't know what you want. It's so hard to tell.

Luke was so different from how Molly had been as a baby. Molly had been full-sized, and she'd come home the day after she was born, pink and healthy with downy golden hair. She had curled her tiny hand closed around Josh's finger, and looked straight up at him with her dreamy clear blue eyes. She had been a peaceful baby, sleeping and feeding easily. She had started to smile at people almost straightaway, and she filled the house with sunshine.

Maybe Luke would be like that one day but it was

hard to imagine. The weird thing was, there were still about three weeks left until the day Luke should have been born. All his life he would be three months older than he should be. At least that wouldn't make any difference to the year he would be in at school, so he would grow up knowing all the same people. It struck Josh that if Luke had been due in November but born in August, rather than due in April and born in January, then in addition to all his other problems he'd have to start school a year early and be the very youngest and smallest – Josh knew *all* about being the smallest – and nobody would ever take into account that the first three months of his life didn't count, and he'd be way behind everyone else and they'd think he was thick.

Molly came running in, suddenly wide-awake and bubbly, and threw herself at her father, who put his coffee cup down hastily, narrowly averting a disaster.

'Easter eggs, Daddy! That's such a good idea!'

'Why – yes, Molly, of course we'll have Easter eggs.' Dad looked slightly bewildered by this onslaught. 'Don't we always?'

'We'll put them all over the house, and soon it will be Easter!' Molly said happily. 'I'll fetch some baskets from school. Can we buy some little tiny ones today at the supermarket?'

'Erm – yes, if you like,' said their father, though Josh could tell he hadn't really grasped what she was talking about. This happened a great deal with Molly.

'Did you find the hairbrush?' Josh asked her, although he could see perfectly well that she hadn't. Molly clapped her hand over her mouth dramatically. She had forgotten all about the hairbrush; something else had caught her attention. This, also, happened a great deal with Molly. She would simply drop whatever she was doing if something more interesting turned up. You could send her off on an errand but the chances of her coming back were tiny.

And now it was time to leave for school, and Molly's hair would just have to stay messed up until they went shopping.

It was raining at break, which was good because it meant they were allowed to stay in the classroom. Josh was almost invisible at the back, tucked in behind Carrie and Bethany, his very own human barricade. Just as long as they didn't wander off to talk in some other part of the room. There were a couple of other girls, Lucy and Kiara, with whom they were really friendly. But this time Josh got lucky; Lucy and Kiara came over to join Carrie and Bethany. This was excellent. A *double* human barricade.

In any case, Shane Walters seemed today to have turned his attentions to William Beresford, the new boy. William Beresford had turned out to be some kind of genius. It was just as well he hadn't taken Claudio's old seat, next to Josh. They'd have had nothing to say to each other. Josh felt stupid just being in the same *room* as William. He could do double-figure multiplication sums in his head, he played the tuba and he was brilliant at games. Thinking games, not ball games. At this very moment he was sitting all by himself with a chessboard. Every so often he would move a piece, turn the board round and look at it from the other side. Josh had never seen anything like it in his life.

'Right, listen, everybody,' said Miss Hollis from the front of the room. 'I'm just going to the staff room to get a drink. I'll be back in two minutes, and I'm leaving the door open, and if Mr Bailey hears any noise he'll be in here in a flash! Got that?'

'Yes, Miss Hollis,' everyone chanted. Miss Hollis left the room, flashing Shane Walters a particularly dark look as she passed him.

William Beresford pushed a black piece forward three squares, turned the board around and surveyed the new position. Josh could see that Shane Walters and his chief sidekick Dylan Brasher were visibly bursting with loathing of him. There was a brief whispered conference; Dylan Brasher took off his left shoe. Josh slid down a few inches further in his seat, watching through the gaps between the girls. Suddenly something went flying through the air, hit William Beresford smack on the face and fell down onto the chessboard, knocking over most of the pieces.

A sudden silence spread around the room as everyone turned to look.

William picked the thing up. It was Dylan Brasher's left sock. Rolled up into a tight little ball.

Josh tried not to think how horrible it must be to have your face so near to Dylan Brasher's sock. To have actually made contact with something that only seconds before had been clinging to Dylan Brasher's stinking sweaty foot.

William Beresford looked at the sock for a few moments. Then he got up, went to the art cupboard, took out a pair of scissors, unrolled the sock and very carefully cut it in half. He threw it in the bin and went back to his seat.

The room was still hushed in awe when Miss Hollis returned with a cup of coffee. 'Goodness,' she said. 'I know I told you to be quiet but I didn't think you'd take me this seriously.' There were a few nervous giggles, and gradually the normal buzz of conversation resumed.

Carrie Lindwell turned round to Josh. 'They're going to kill him at lunchtime,' she said. Lucy and Kiara had slipped back to their seats, which were just across the aisle from William Beresford. Probably they wanted to take a last look at him.

Josh nodded.

'Do you think we ought to tell someone?'

'No,' said Josh. What was the point? If they didn't kill him today, they'd kill him tomorrow. Or some other day. And at least it kept their minds off Josh.

'Did you have a look at Technomon?' Bethany asked. It was a deadly swift and sudden change of subject, but Josh had been expecting this question to be asked at some point and had his answer all ready.

'I don't really think it's my sort of thing,' he said.

'Oh, Josh. Of course it would be!'

'How do you know unless you look?'

They sounded like his parents! Really, he shouldn't have to put up with this!

'What's the point of it, anyway?' he asked, stalling for time. 'What do you actually *do*?'

'Well, you choose your pet, and it hatches . . .'

'And you feed it, and it grows and learns things . . .'

'And you can teach it tricks . . .'

'And enter it in competitions!'

They were doing the duet thing again.

'Do they breed?'

'Nooooo!' chorused the girls, pulling faces of disgust. 'You know that never happens!' said Carrie.

'Well, *that's* not true,' Josh said. 'In Pokémon Gold and Silver you could breed Pokémon. You could leave two Pokémon at the Day Care Centre, and if they were attracted to each other you could go back in a while and they'd have laid an egg. It was the only way you could ever get hold of some Pokémon types, like . . .' They were looking at him as if to say, 'What a geek!' Josh fell silent.

'My Luponio won a race last week!' said Bethany, smoothly changing the subject. Josh almost asked if her Luponio was turning into a wolf or a horse, but bit his tongue just in time. 'And I've trained it to jump fences!' Bethany added. That seemed to settle the question.

'And my Forkfoot is studying circus skills!' said Carrie. 'But you can do whatever you want. You can make them into fighters if you like. But you'd better pick the right type.' Josh didn't doubt it. Just imagine trying to teach a Glostrich, one of those super-vain birds, to fight. It would squeal and run away and find a beauty parlour to hide in. Perhaps the Glostrich had special attacks it could learn, called things like Shampoo Spray Gun, Feather Flap and Nuclear Hair Bomb. He could just imagine it now, challenging a Glostrich with a *good* fighter – a dragon, say – and the Glostrich coming at you with a pink lipstick, and you set your dragon to Flame Blast and it went *whooooosh!* and the Glostrich's feathers would catch fire and it would roll over screaming and . . .

No!

Josh knew they'd only told him about fighting because they thought it was what a boy would like. And look at how he'd started to think straightaway! How did girls *do* that?

And anyway, what was he doing even thinking about this? Had Technomon actually got to him?

Thank heavens he hadn't said anything out loud. Talking was the dangerous thing. As long as you didn't get sucked into talking, you could keep yourself safe.

5

'So anyway, at lunchtime they caught him outside the toilets and they gave him such a thumping his glasses got broken. And then his mum came to the school and she was furious, and Shane Walters and Dylan Brasher got suspended.'

'Boys are so *mean*,' said Molly, her face crumpling with alarm.

'Girls can be mean,' Josh said, though he knew what she meant. When girls were mean the results were rarely so physically painful.

Their father, sitting in the driver's seat, was frowning. 'Do these boys often behave like this, Josh?'

'They're pretty bad,' Josh said. 'They've got worse this year.' Josh suspected they would carry on getting worse as they grew bigger and bigger. 'They're going to a different school from me in September,' he said, in case his father was thinking the same thing.

His father said, 'Hmmm.' And then took a sharp left into the entrance of the supermarket.

'Can we have a drink before we do the shopping?' Josh asked.

'And a cake!' said Molly, bounding around in delight just at the thought of it.

'We don't want to be too long,' their father said, looking suddenly anxious. 'Your mother's all on her own with Luke.'

'But Dad. They'll both be asleep. This is the time of day Luke sleeps the most. She'll be *glad* if we stay out longer. She hates it when we wake him up.'

'Hmmm,' Dad said again. And then: 'Actually, you've probably got a good point there. But let's do the shopping first and get it out of the way.'

'You can't do it that way,' Josh said patiently. 'All the ice cream will melt.' Did his father know nothing about shopping at all?

'We're buying ice cream?'

'Yes!' said Molly, dancing backwards. 'Eighteen different kinds. Chip Chop Choc and Crunchy Biscuit and Strawberry Surprise and Fuzzy Monkey and . . . '

'*Fuzzy Monkey?*'

'It's *Funky* Monkey,' said Josh. 'Basically it's banana.'

'Oh, well then, clearly we can't do without it,' said Dad, not putting up any great resistance as they steered him firmly to the supermarket café.

Josh and Molly both had a Sprite and a chocolate cake, and their father chose coffee and a doughnut. Josh was enjoying this outing. It was nice, just being the three of them. This thought gave him a sudden pang of guilt. Of course it would be wonderful if Mum and Luke were here as well, and they were all together. Except – except. Mum and Luke would change the whole atmosphere. Luke had so many problems and needed so much attention that you could never really relax when he was around. The heavy weight of worry seemed to press down on all of them.

They did a *huge* shopping spree. Josh couldn't remember ever buying so much stuff at one go. The carriers wouldn't all fit in the trolley, and Josh and Molly had to walk alongside carefully on the way to the car, holding the top layer in place. Molly had added quite a lot of non-essential items, mostly chocolate-based, and including at least five bags of sugar-coated miniature chocolate eggs, but Dad had been in an indulgent mood and had let her have pretty much anything she wanted.

On the drive home she was prattling happily away in the back about Easter baskets and painting Easter eggs and how she'd got a new reading book which was the last of the red ones and when she'd finished it she could start on the orange ones. Dad laughed and asked how many different colours there were to get through, and Molly told him seven, it was the Rainbow reading scheme and you did the books in order of the colours of the rainbow, and did he want to hear her read tonight? And Dad said he couldn't think of anything he'd like more.

They were all feeling light-hearted when they got back home.

'Your groceries delivered to your door, madam!' Dad said with a sweeping bow, but their mother didn't seem at all pleased. 'Where have you been? I thought you'd be back half an hour ago! I've been worried!'

'We just stopped for a quick drink,' said Dad, looking somewhat flattened by this welcome. 'We thought you'd be resting . . .'

'Luke hasn't slept more than fifteen minutes all day!

When do you think I get a chance to rest?' She looked lined and drawn with worry and tiredness. All the sense of fun that had been flowing between Dad and Josh and Molly evaporated on the instant.

Their father put the shopping away, while Josh set a huge saucepan of water on to boil ready for spaghetti. Molly, meanwhile, had laid her little bags of chocolate eggs out on the table. She had grabbed them as they slid down on the conveyor belt at the checkout, and packed them up together. Now she had produced a stack of little wicker baskets and was sorting the eggs by colour.

'What are you doing, Molly?' Josh asked her.

'This is how we're going to carry on with the Easter egg hunting,' Molly said. 'This will be the best fun. Everybody sit down and I'll show you. Sit *down*, Mum.'

Their mother sat down, looking at the eggs in puzzlement.

'Dad, sit down.'

'Moll, I'm still busy unpacking. You press on. I'll be listening to every word.'

'All right. Now. Mum, these are your eggs.' She pushed a basket of blue eggs across the table. 'Dad, you have the pink ones.'

'My *very* favourite colour,' said their father, stacking cans in a cupboard.

'Josh can have the mauve ones and I'll have yellow. Luke's too young to play so we'll save the green ones for Easter to eat.'

Josh looked down sourly at his basket. 'What are we

supposed to do with these? I'm not playing if it's something stupid.'

'Give her a chance, old man,' said Dad.

'What we do is hide them all around the house, and you keep your basket, and when you find an egg that isn't your colour, you take it and put it in your basket!'

Oh God, thought Josh. This was starting to sound agonising. Let's sing a happy happy Easter bunny song, tra la la. 'It's weeks till Easter yet,' he said, grumpily. 'What's the point of doing this now?'

'Well, Mummy and Daddy started it!' Molly said.

'We what?' said Mum.

'Actually,' said Dad, standing up and shutting the freezer door, 'this is the best time to start, because that way we can have three weeks of fun! A three-week long hunt!'

Molly gazed at him in rapture.

'But we'll find all the eggs long before then,' said Josh. 'We'll find most of them straightaway.'

Molly's face fell.

'But why hide them all at once?' asked Dad. 'If we all hide two or three a day, people will still be finding them for ages. And nobody will ever know when a few more have been hidden. Nobody will know how many are lying around unfound at any moment. It will be an everlasting treasure hunt.'

'Everyone will know when Molly's hidden some,' Josh said. 'She'll be giggling and looking at the door and saying, "Doesn't anybody feel like having a little walk round the house?"'

‘I won’t!’ said Molly indignantly. ‘I never do that!’

‘You do! You can’t keep a secret for five seconds! You . . . ’

‘Stop squabbling,’ said their father, throwing the last empty carrier bag in the bin with an expression of triumph. ‘Molly, I think it’s a wonderful idea. It’s time we all relaxed and had some family fun, now Luke’s safe and home with us.’

Their mother smiled, though you could see that she wasn’t excited by the thought of hunting for Easter eggs.

Josh looked at his mauve eggs again and shrugged. He wished it hadn’t been Molly’s idea. As her older brother it was his duty to tell Molly all her ideas were stupid. His father flashed him a pleading look that said: ‘I know what you’re thinking. But our family needs this right now. Be nice.’

Josh sighed. It would, certainly, be good for the family to have something else going on in the house.

‘OK, I’ll play,’ he said, getting to his feet and setting off with his basket.

‘Are you going to hide some eggs now?’ Molly asked, her face all lit up with excitement.

‘That would be telling,’ said Josh, and disappeared.

Josh hid his basket in a bedroom drawer. If he left it out in the open Molly would find them and count the eggs, and he’d bet anything she knew how many he’d started with. Then, after tea, when his sister had stopped watching him quite so closely, he decided to hide three mauve eggs. He hoped his parents were going to play properly, and not leave all the eggs for him and Molly to find.

He perched the first on a ball of cotton wool behind the shampoo in the bathroom. Mum would probably find that one. The second egg he slipped into Molly's favourite breakfast cereal. It would tumble into her bowl in the morning. He had planned to hide the third one, which was meant for his father, in the computer room, but Molly was in there already, curled up on the floor with her yellow eggs and the unused green ones, arranging them in patterns on the Technomon mousemat.

'Have you been hiding eggs?' she asked straightaway and 'Who knows?' Josh replied. He sat down at the computer and checked his e-mail, in case Claudio had written. For the first few weeks after Claudio had gone back to Italy they'd swapped e-mails almost every day, but gradually the intervals between Josh's e-mails and Claudio's replies had stretched longer and longer. Now he was lucky to hear from Claudio once a week. Josh knew what had happened. Claudio came from a very large family. Hundreds of people, friends and relations, had been waiting in Italy for his return. He was back at his old school and his memories of Josh were fading by the minute. Probably in a few more months' time he'd have forgotten him altogether.

Josh had no e-mails waiting. He shrugged.

Perhaps he'd have a quick game of DX-Ball. If Molly would only go away he could hide his third egg, but if he said anything, she'd guess what he was up to and be back in the room a minute later, searching for a mauve egg. Restless, he spun the chair around – it was onc of those swivelly office chairs that are brilliant for spinning – and as he spun he noticed another of the little wicker baskets, sitting on the windowsill by the computer table. This one contained a single egg, larger than the sugar-coated treasure hunt eggs. It was painted in luridly bright, improbable colours like something out of a Disney film: bright blue, with purple splodges. Of course – he remembered now. Molly was painting eggs at school. This would be one of them.

'What's *this* doing here?'

'That was the *first* egg. Isn't it lovely? I think they meant it for you, though. It was sitting on your picture.'

'What?' It had happened again. Two sentences into a conversation with Molly and he was completely lost.

'It was on the floor when I found it. On top of this.' She pointed at the mousemat. 'I picked it up in case a dog came in and ate it.'

'Molly, we don't have a dog.'

'Maybe a dog would come visiting. Or a cat might have jumped in the window,' Molly said, collecting up all her yellow eggs and replacing them in their basket.

'Molly, you painted this egg at school.'

'No I didn't. I told you! I found it here this morning!'

'But it's in one of your baskets.'

'I put it in there just now. I picked it up off the floor this morning.'

'Well, where do you think it came from then?'

'Mummy and Daddy, of course,' said Molly. Josh sighed. Did she really not understand that both of their parents were much too tired and preoccupied to do things like that any more? And then he thought – well, yes, she does realise that, and that's why she's taken it on herself to organise this egg hunting. She must have planted this egg of her own and pretended to believe it was from her parents, to make them feel guilty and kickstart them into hiding eggs themselves. It was quite clever. He hadn't realised that girls started to be tricky at such a young age.

'I'm going to have a quick hunt around,' said Molly, leaving him alone at last. Finally he had a chance to hide his third egg. Now, where should he put it? The computer and the terminal and the speakers didn't offer any good hiding places. They were big things with flat surfaces. What you needed were nooks and crannies. He could put it in a drawer but that wasn't exactly creative. He wanted to do better than that.

Suddenly he had a thought. Where was the last place anyone would look for a hidden egg?

The answer was: inside an egg basket! Because people would think, well, obviously nobody would hide a thing inside the place it was supposed to be.

He would just tuck the little mauve egg in with Molly's big blue and purple one, and he would bet absolutely anything it wouldn't be found for days.

He was just arranging the basket when he had such a tremendous shock that he almost dropped the whole lot on the floor.

The big blue and purple egg had vibrated against his hand. And even as he stared at it now, it made a distinct movement to the right and then rolled back to the left, as if an invisible hand were gently shaking it.

The egg was alive.

6

Josh collected his wits, and recovered from his fright almost straightaway. It wasn't like an apple doing a turnover or a banana doing the splits. It was an egg, and eggs could be alive. It was highly, highly unusual. Freakishly unusual. But it wasn't impossible, and so there was no reason to find it scary.

Somehow or other, a living egg had got in with the other eggs at Molly's school and she'd painted it and brought it home. She hadn't noticed anything, because the chick inside hadn't grown big enough yet to start moving around.

Josh very nearly got up and ran out to show everybody. But then he stopped and thought again. When this egg hatched, there would be a tiny baby chick in an Easter basket. Surrounded by little eggs! There was only one little egg there at the moment, but Josh could add several more. And just imagine Molly's face when she saw it! She'd think a miracle had happened. It would be the most thrilling thing ever in her entire life.

He would organise it for her. It would be his surprise.

Josh carried the egg in its basket upstairs to his room, and closed the door very firmly.

The egg gave one more little wiggle and then fell still. How long was all this going to take? Josh was woefully ignorant on the subject of egg hatching, but his instincts told him that once the chick was strong enough to set the egg wobbling and shaking, it wouldn't be so very much longer until it was able to crack the shell and bash its way out.

He sat quite still for half an hour, watching. During the first ten minutes the egg only moved very occasionally, but by the end it was moving almost as much of the time as it was still.

Josh couldn't remember ever in his life sitting so still for so long, doing nothing, just watching. He couldn't bear to take his eyes off the egg for even one second. What if the first crack appeared while he wasn't looking? He had never seen an egg hatch in real life. You saw it all the time on television, but that wasn't the same thing.

And then, after another fifteen minutes of increasing activity, a crack *did* appear, just a tiny crack, maybe a centimetre long. Josh clapped his hand over his mouth and held his breath. This was *it*!

But no – there followed another long interval of wriggling movement that achieved nothing. It was as if the chick hadn't noticed the place where it had made the crack, and instead of working at the same spot it was bashing away randomly somewhere else.

'Here!' said Josh, tapping his finger very gently over the crack. There was a brief silence while the chick thought about this. And then a sudden enthusiastic kick in exactly the right place sent the crack shooting wider.

Who ever said chicks were stupid?

There was a pause while the chick got its strength back. With its next effort it chipped off a triangular piece of shell. Josh could actually see a leg now, pushing away beneath the thin membrane that remained. He gazed as if hypnotised as it kicked and kicked again; the shell broke wide open at last and a tiny pale pink creature coated in gunk crawled out, making faint high-pitched cheeping noises.

Josh gasped. And then drew backwards.

It didn't look like anything like Josh imagined a newborn chick.

The creature shook itself, sneezed, half-opened its gummy eyes and began to wriggle and kick feebly. Josh supposed it was trying to find its feet. It had only been born for about twenty seconds and it probably hadn't worked out yet which way was up and which was down, let alone where its legs were.

But as he watched, Josh began to feel deeply uneasy. He was almost certain now that this was not a chick. Even if chicks were born pale pink, which he supposed was possible if they hadn't started to grow their feathers yet, this – this thing – was entirely the wrong shape to be a bird. It looked more like a lizard. Did lizards hatch from eggs? His brain wasn't working properly. Lizards – were reptiles. Of course they hatched from eggs. Everything did, except for mammals.

How could Molly have got hold of a *reptile* egg? Were they breeding them at the Infants school? It seemed wildly unlikely. The word *reptile* suddenly sounded very dark and sneaky and sinister. Why had he never noticed that before? It was a horrible word. *Lizard* wasn't so bad.

Except that this creature didn't in all honesty look all that much like a lizard, either.

But it had to be a lizard. What else could it be?

As Josh stared at it, feeling the first twinges of real fear, the lizard finally staggered to its feet. The wicker basket promptly toppled over. The lizard tumbled forward onto the carpet with a series of panicky little cheeps, and immediately set about getting back on its feet again. Four feet. Four legs.

Josh suddenly had a flashback to the film *Jurassic Park*, and baby dinosaurs smashing their way out of eggs and growing up to be velociraptors.

The lizard was already gaining confidence in the use of its limbs, and, with some determination, it began to stumble across the carpet towards Josh. The slimy birth coating was coming off its body onto the carpet, leaving a trail like a slug. Josh could see tiny hair-thin blood vessels and flecks of yellow.

He backed away into a corner. The lizard stopped in its tracks, considered this, gave what sounded like a miniature sigh, turned itself around so that it was facing Josh again, and continued tottering its wobbly uncertain way towards him.

Half of Josh wanted to scream as loudly as he could, leap over the creature, run out of the room and slam the door behind him.

And at the same time, a voice was saying in his head: *Coward*. Whatever it was, it was less than three inches long. How could it possibly hurt him?

But why did it keep coming for him, scrabbling its

way so doggedly across the carpet in his direction? Why be so persistent, if it didn't mean him harm?

Suddenly Josh realised that there was another, entirely opposite, possibility. He had heard all about newborn ducklings who attached themselves to the first living thing they saw.

Perhaps this lizard thought Josh was his mother.

He felt a faint stirring of tenderness. It was so very small and helpless, and now it wasn't quite so slimy it was a great deal better-looking. It was almost cute.

But once you have thought the word *velociraptor* it is surprisingly difficult to banish it altogether from your mind. Josh gulped. Then he took a sock and rolled it up over his right hand. He rolled the end down again so he was protected by a double thickness of sock. Then, summoning up all the courage he had, he put his hand out on the floor, offering it to the lizard. He had absolutely no idea what would happen next.

The lizard stopped, made a noise that sounded like a very faint OOOF, and sniffed at the sock. Josh winced. He was certain his feet smelled better than Dylan Brasher's, but this was a day-old sock just the same. Absurdly, he found himself mentally apologising that he hadn't been able to find a clean one.

But the lizard didn't seem to mind. It stretched out a tiny front leg, touched the sock and curled its foot round with a surprisingly tight grip. Josh's hand started to shake. He couldn't control it. Now there were two feet pulling at the sock. And in no time at all, the little creature had clawed its way up to the very centre of

Josh's palm, where it stopped, and gazed up at him with a pair of bright green eyes. Not fierce eyes, not evil eyes, but eyes that said: There! See what I can do! Aren't you proud of me?

And then it opened its mouth wide and gave a squeak. Josh could see right to the top of its throat and all he saw was gum.

No teeth.

It was time to be brave.

Josh put out his left hand, his pink, naked, bare, unprotected left hand, next to the right one, cupping them together. The lizard looked at it for a few moments, and then dragged its tiny scaly body across. It gave a little sigh of contentment and collapsed in exhaustion in Josh's left palm, as if to be this close to Josh was all it had wanted, and now it could finally curl up and relax.

Josh sat quite still for some minutes, just looking at it. A million thoughts were flashing through his mind, but the one that kept rising to the surface was how ridiculous it was to have been afraid. He, Josh, could crush this creature with one movement of his hand. *It* was the one who had the right to be afraid. And here it was, half-dozing as it recovered from its journey. It trusted him completely. If it was a cat it would have been purring.

Josh stretched out a tentative finger and stroked its wings. (*Wings?*) The lizard made that OOOF! sound again, sneezed and rubbed its head against Josh's finger.

'You *do* think I'm your mother,' Josh said softly. 'I'm going to have to take care of you, aren't I? I don't know where you came from, and I don't know what you are, and this isn't going to be easy. But I'll do my best. OK?'

Cheep, said the lizard contentedly, as if it had understood every word, and as Josh tickled its wings gently, which sent it rolling over in ecstasies of bliss, and as he ran his fingers over the still-soft newborn scales, it became impossible to pretend to himself any longer that he didn't know it was a dragon.

7

There were so many practical things that needing seeing to, urgently, that Josh simply didn't have the time to stop right now and think about what had happened. Which was just as well, because if he was going crazy, or the world was turning inside out – and there didn't seem to be too many other possibilities – thinking about it wasn't going to help. He'd probably end up screaming or climbing up the curtains – or both – and the dragon would be taken away and he'd never see it again. He had to keep calm.

Josh placed the dragon very gently in one of his clothes drawers. 'Now, you just sit there like a good... boy' – Josh couldn't quite bring himself to say the word 'dragon' aloud – 'while I fetch you some things. OK?' The dragon gazed up at him and gave a weak cheep of distress, as if to say, 'No! Please don't leave me on my own!'

Aw heck. 'I'll be very quick,' Josh said. 'I promise!' The dragon made the sad sound again. It was heart-breaking. Josh steeled himself and pushed the drawer in, leaving a gap of an inch. He couldn't bring himself to shut it all the way, leaving the dragon in the dark. It might be terrified of the dark. It couldn't possibly climb out. Could it? No, of course it couldn't. It had only just learned to walk.

Josh slipped out, closing the door firmly behind him.

Astonishing to think that the rest of the world had been carrying on as usual. It had been no more than an hour since he took the egg up to his room, though it felt like several lifetimes. In the old days Josh would never have been left to his own devices for a whole hour. His mother would have come up to find out where he was, to check that he was OK. But now... now you could get away with things. With almost anything you wanted.

There was crying coming from an upstairs room – Luke, making a noise that was louder and more agonised than his usual general miserable grumbling cry. Josh suddenly realised that this had been going on for some time now. Somehow he had heard it without noticing that he had heard.

Downstairs, Dad was brushing Molly's hair with one of the two new brushes they'd bought at the supermarket, while she read aloud to him from her new red Rainbow schoolbook. Josh paused for a moment to look at them. Such a cosy, normal scene. Such a picture of domestic contentment. Such a normal happy family. Provided that you forgot about the baby upstairs screaming its lungs out – oh, and of course the simple matter of the dragon in the bedroom drawer.

His father waved at him. 'Hi there. Luke seems a bit poorly, so your mother's taken him upstairs.'

'Oh – right,' said Josh, and headed off to the kitchen, leaving them to it. He needed some kind of a box. A cardboard box would be best, but a hasty search of the kitchen and the area outside the back door turned up nothing suitable. Then he spotted a large plastic ice cream tub, lying right at the top of the rubbish in the bin. It wasn't perfect, but it would have to do. He rinsed and dried the tub, and the lid as well. He didn't think the dragon would be able to scramble out of the tub – it was three or even four times the dragon's height – but better to be safe than sorry. Who knew what he might need?

He bashed six air holes into the lid, and grabbed one of Luke's undrunk bottles of milk. At least in this household there was never any shortage of baby food, though he had no idea what baby dragons required. Was milk just for mammals? Did lizards start out drinking milk? Did fish? Did birds? He couldn't remember. His brain had turned to sawdust. He found two jam jar lids and took those as well, to use as feeding bowls.

He ran back upstairs and collected a handful of cotton wool balls from the bathroom. If only they had a small pet, a hamster or a gerbil! Then there would be proper bedding and sawdust. But they had no pets at all, and so this would have to do.

'I'm back,' he said, closing his bedroom door, rushing over to the drawer and easing it out.

The dragon was gone.

Josh gave a yelp of horror, and began to rummage frantically through the clothes in the drawer, shaking them out and hurling them into a pile on the floor behind him, until the drawer lay empty.

How could he have been so stupid as to take his eyes off it for one single second? It was the most amazing thing to happen to him in his entire life, and now it was gone. Josh looked helplessly around. It could be anywhere. His room was in a terrible mess, and there were hundreds of hiding places. Any time he opened the bedroom door the dragon could slip out and be lost forever. If it wasn't lost already.

If he hadn't imagined the whole thing.

Josh got down on his knees and peered under the bed. He squinted into the narrow gap under the wardrobe. He began to pull out the chest of drawers to look behind it, but froze as he realised it was too dangerous. He might run the dragon over and squash it to death. There was no way to do a proper search for something so very small, without putting it in danger.

And then: *Cheeeep!*

It came from somewhere in the pile of clothes. The wave of joy and relief that flooded right through Josh was so strong he felt the sharp sting of tears.

'OK,' he said softly. 'You're safe. I'll find you.' He picked up the jumper on top, opened it out flat, peeked inside, gently shook it. Nothing.

Cheeeep!

The dragon was in the second pair of trousers. It had burrowed its way down to the very bottom of the right-hand pocket. At the sight of Josh it started to squeak so loudly that for a moment he was almost afraid somebody might hear.

'Hush!' he said, lifting the dragon up in his cupped hands. 'You have to be more careful! I thought I'd lost you! I was worried sick!'

Cheeeeeeep! said the dragon, opening its mouth as

wide as it could, and all at once Josh realised that the noise wasn't just one of affection. The dragon had never been fed, and it was hungry.

Josh arranged the cotton wool balls into a comfortable fluffy bed, pink and orange and white, and popped the dragon into its new home to try it out while he prepared the milk, squeezing it from Luke's bottle into one of the jam jar lids. 'Here you are,' he said coaxingly, placing the lid down near the dragon's nose. 'Come and try this. It's good.' He hoped against hope that the dragon would be able to feed itself, because although it had a wide jaw for its size the rubber teat at the end of Luke's bottle was far, far too big. It was bigger than the dragon's entire head.

The dragon took a huge gulp of milk, spluttered and sneezed. Milk bubbles blew out of its nostrils and its face crumpled with shock.

'*Greedy*,' said Josh. 'Little sips to start with. Try again.'

The dragon had another go, approaching with more caution, and this time it managed to keep most of the milk down. It climbed into the feeding bowl and sat down in the middle to drink, which wasn't exactly what Josh had in mind. He made a mental note to get the dragon a container of water for paddling and bathing.

The dragon made a comical sight, splashing around in the milk, but it hadn't really drunk a great deal, and after a few minutes it was sick.

Josh sighed. Perhaps the milk wasn't so good after all.

The only other person who drank it was Luke, and it made him sick too. Perhaps he should try regular milk. Or – chocolate milk. They'd bought a litre bottle today. Why not? Any sensible creature would prefer chocolate milk to powdered baby milk. Josh fetched some.

The dragon certainly seemed to like this better, though it was impossible to prevent it from climbing in and splashing, and Josh doubted very much whether it had taken enough nourishment. But its immediate hunger pangs seemed to have been eased, and he could try something else tomorrow. Because it was already half past ten, and even though the next day was Saturday he really ought to get to bed. And so must the dragon.

It was lucky that Josh's bed wasn't tucked away in a corner. There was a gap on the far side, the side away from the door, and so he could hide the ice cream tub away where nobody coming in would see it. 'Bedtime,' he said. He climbed into his pyjamas, tiptoed to the door and listened. Luke was still crying, but the sound came from downstairs now. He went to the top of the stairs, and heard adult voices murmuring below. They were *both* still up. He would have to be careful. Only when everyone was tucked up in bed asleep would it be safe to take the dragon out and play with it on the bed. Otherwise someone might barge in at any second to say, 'Aren't you asleep yet?' – and that would spell disaster.

The dragon seemed tired, in any case, and disinclined to play. Josh allowed it to kiss him goodnight, which it did by blowing warm breath through its nostrils onto Josh's nose. Josh huffed a breath back to it, which made it squirm with delight. He felt quite proud of himself. He was mastering the basics of dragon communication already.

'I must think of a name for you,' he whispered to the dragon as it curled up on its cotton wool bed and began to snooze. 'Flame?' No – that was *much* too obvious. How about Firecracker? Or Thunderblast? Firestorm? These were all very fine and ferocious names but they seemed a bit outlandish for such a tiny creature. Maybe he'd grow into one of them in time, but at present it would sound like a joke, like when you called someone huge Tiny. Or, indeed, when you called a premature baby Goliath.

Perhaps he should call it Mr Burns, like Mr Burns in 'The Simpsons'. He was still chuckling about this when he dozed off, only to be awoken minutes later by frantic *cheeps* from below.

Josh was to get very little rest that night. The dragon wouldn't sleep in the dark, so Josh had to put his bedside light down on the floor beside its den. And that meant every time he looked down he *saw* the dragon brightly lit, and he couldn't resist picking it up and taking it into bed with him just for one minute. The dragon adored this, and immediately set about making itself comfortable, burrowing into Josh's neck, turning round a few times and then falling fast asleep. It couldn't make it any plainer that it wanted to snuggle up with Josh, not on its own in an ice cream tub. 'No, you *can't* sleep there,' Josh had to say, over and over again. 'I'm not your mother! No I'm *not*! I might squash you in the night.

Back you go.' And the dragon would give him a mournful look as if to say, 'Well, why not leave me where I was then?' which Josh supposed was fair enough.

And all the time, he could hear his brother crying. Was it always this bad? He knew Luke wasn't a good sleeper but tonight he seemed to be screaming and sobbing the whole night through.

And so Josh tossed and turned, drifting in and out of sleep and only half certain what was a dream and what wasn't.

Because the most probable answer to the mystery of the dragon was that he had dreamed it.

Working out if you're dreaming or not is fiendishly tricky. If you're not dreaming you know you're not. The problem is, even when you *are* dreaming you know you're not. But his mother, who had the weirdest dreams all the time, had found out a trick that always worked and taught it to him.

If you want to know whether you're dreaming, you have to find something written down and read it. Look away, and then look back. If you're dreaming, the words will have changed. Josh had tried this maybe two hundred times over the last three years, and once, just once out of the two hundred, the words did indeed change. He had caught himself dreaming! It was the most amazing sensation. He was so shocked that he woke up immediately, and ran into his parents' room to tell his mother, who was too busy dreaming to hear. He could see her lips move as she mouthed dreamwords in silence.

Josh had been having the wackiest dreams himself since Luke had been born. Some of them had been quite disturbing. He'd dreamed that his brother was twin girls called May and Delilah, and that he'd been born two years old (though looking like a giant baby, not like a two-year-old). He'd dreamed that the doctors said they'd have to put Luke back for three months, that Luke had an electronic voice controlled by a computer, that he came home in a wheelchair.

He had dreamed that Luke was dead.

He'd never before had Luke-dreams involving eggs hatching, but you could see that there was a possible connection. Josh took a look at his sleeping dragon, got out of bed and climbed across the mountains of clothes and other junk on the floor to fetch a book to do the dream test, though he knew perfectly well that the fact that he had to use a book at all was a bad omen. In Josh's dreams there were always signs and notices pinned up all over the walls, and even if they weren't there in the first place all he had to do was think of them and they would appear. The bedroom walls remained stubbornly bare. It would have to be the book. *Circle of Doom*, he read. He looked away, counted to five and looked back. It said *Circle of Doom*.

That was that, then. Not a dream.

The only other possibility was magic.

Josh had completely given up believing in magic. Molly still believed. She believed in witches and wizards, in talking ghosts, in fairy dust and space dust, in elves and pixies . . . and dragons. Molly thought that if you dropped a coin in a wishing well your wish would come true. She was certain that Loopy Rose the space cucumber, not to mention the chocolate seahorse family, had their own private languages, and that if a person only studied hard enough they could learn to make themselves invisible or to fly. And all her life Josh had done his duty as an older brother, by telling her on every possible occasion that she was bonkers.

And now something had happened that knocked away the foundations of everything Josh had thought he knew about the world. He had fallen through a wormhole into Molly's universe. Now he was tumbling through hyperspace into the unknown, and he wasn't sure that anyone would be there to catch him when he landed.

8

'Josh! Josh, are you still in bed?' There was a clattering on the landing and his sister burst into his room, all chirpy and tousled and bouncing with exhilarated Saturday-morning freedom. 'Thank you for the egg you put in my cereal box! I've got four now! You have to come down for breakfast. We've called you twice already.'

'Errrrghh.' Josh forced his eyes open with difficulty. He had finally fallen into a fitful sleep, and he wanted to carry on sleeping for at least another ten hours undisturbed. Maybe twenty hours. He had a vague recollection of hiding a mauve egg in Molly's favourite cereal for her to find, but that seemed to belong in another lifetime, to a Josh who had been an entirely different person, a Josh who was now a fading memory of a universe where things made sense.

A small squeaky sound came from the floor on the left of the bed. Josh wasn't the only one to have been woken by Molly's abrupt entrance. He sat bolt upright, as if to create a barrier.

Cheeep.

Molly frowned. 'Who's that? I heard a voice.'

'No you didn't, stupid. It's the bedsprings.' He climbed out of bed and crossed the room to the door, to block her from coming in any further. 'I'll be down in two minutes. Off you go. Now! Go!' Molly backed out, eyes wide with surprise. Josh rarely showed any signs of being pleased to see her, but even so it wasn't like him to be *quite* this unfriendly.

Josh picked up the dragon's box and put it on the bed. It was a discouraging sight. There was a nasty brown mess on the cotton wool bedding where it had been sprayed with chocolate-coloured sick during the night, and some shinier, greeny-black patches that couldn't be anything other than dragon poo. The box gave off a rich sickly smell that was somehow sour and sweet at the same time.

'You couldn't keep the chocolate milk down either?' Josh's heart sank. The dragon looked bedraggled and forlorn. It needed proper dragon food, it had been lying in its own vomit all night and the cheeps it was making were distinctly half-hearted compared to the night before. It was hungry and miserable, and all of this was Josh's fault.

'But I don't know what to do!' he said in desperation, tickling the dragon softly behind the ears. 'It's not that I'm not trying. I can't tell what you need!' The dragon looked away, avoiding his eye, as if it didn't trust him any more but was too basically well-mannered to say so.

'I'll fetch some new stuff for you to try eating and drinking. We'll find the right thing eventually. And I'll change all your dirty bedding and your water. Everything nice and clean. You'll feel much better. And we'll find you some toys to play with, OK? So just hang in there.' It was fighting talk, but deep down Josh knew that if he couldn't find something the dragon could digest soon, all the toys and clean beds in the world weren't going to make a lickety split of difference.

Breakfast was scrambled eggs and toast. 'Stone cold!' his mother grumbled, though whether she was grumbling at the toast for being cold or at Josh for being late wasn't clear. 'I'll make some fresh.'

The scrambled eggs looked well past their finest hour also, but they were surely a nourishing food and well worth a try. Toast, on the other hand, would be useless. For toast you needed teeth. He had to try and get hold of things that were soft and soggy. Baby mush. Goo.

'Actually, I was thinking I might quite like some porridge,' he said, knowing as the words left his mouth that he had never in his entire life asked for porridge before, and that even if he did he would never use those careful, stilted, trying-not-to-give-anything-away words. He never talked that way. Even Goldilocks would be ashamed to sound so prissy.

'Porridge?' his mother said, bemused.

'Porridge?' asked his father, who was holding the baby against his left shoulder, rubbing his back in a slow circular motion. Luke was crying, a slow ragged persistent noise of the kind that would drill into your brain if you paid it too much attention. Josh could see that it had drilled into his mother's brain already. She looked faded, wiped-out, as if someone had turned down her brightness control. He wished, briefly, that Luke's volume control could be turned down, and felt ashamed of the thought an instant later.

'He means Oats-You-Like,' said Molly, who had finished eating and was counting out chocolate eggs from her basket. 'We bought some yesterday.'

Josh's mother looked in the cupboard. 'Oh. I see. Chocolate flavour Oats-You-Like. Is that what you want, Josh?'

'Chocolate doesn't seem to work,' Josh said without thinking. He was too tired to concentrate on his words.

'Doesn't *work*? What do you mean?'

'I mean – do we have any other kind?'

'Golden Syrup,' his mother said, rummaging.

'That sounds good. And I'll have a bit of scrambled egg as well, please,' he added hastily, before his mother could scrape it all into the bin.

His father gave him a concerned look. The porridge conversation had caught his attention. 'Are you feeling all right, Josh? Waking you up this morning was like raising the dead, and now you're here you look exhausted. If you were six years older I'd suspect you'd been out on the town with your mates till the early hours. There, there, old son.' This last sentence was addressed to Luke, who was still screeching inconsolably. Most of his face was buried in his father's sweater. The small bit that Josh could see was crumpled up tight and flushed red.

Molly looked up suddenly and said to Josh: 'Where *were* you last night? I didn't even see you!'

'Busy,' Josh muttered. The microwave went *ping* and his hot oat cereal arrived. 'And I didn't sleep so well. Luke was crying.' Every word of this was true, although he had left out all the vital details.

'Luke had a dreadful night,' his father said. 'I think he's got indigestion.'

'We're going out for a drive in a moment,' Molly said.

'Who are?'

'Me and you and Luke and Daddy.'

Josh's jaw dropped. He hadn't started to consider the rest of the day yet, and now it seemed people had been planning it all out without him. 'Who said?'

'Luke usually settles down in the car,' said Dad. 'The rhythm of the engine soothes him. It's always worked with every baby I've known. So I thought we'd go out for a long drive and let your mother catch up on her sleep. We could go over to the lakes.'

This was the last thing Josh wanted.

'Actually I think I'd better not go,' he said.

Everyone stared at him.

'Why not?' his father asked. He looked taken aback and more than a little hurt.

'I need to tidy my room!' Josh said desperately. 'It's in a terrible mess!'

Everyone stared even harder, and Josh shrank in the face of their disbelief.

'He's definitely ill,' his father said, eventually.

'Yes!' Josh said. 'Ill! I feel sick. If I went in the car I'd just be worse!' Why on earth hadn't he said this in the first place?

'I don't want him being sick in the car!' his mother said, to Josh's relief. 'Remember what it was like? You never get the smell out.' This was a big issue in the Harper family. Molly had been carsick all her life until about a year ago, and it was true that the smell had never really left the car. In Josh's memory it was all mixed up with the smell of petrol at filling stations, a rich and noxious combination that was so overpowering it had sometimes made him sick as well. His father had got a new car last summer, after Molly had grown out of being carsick and before they'd known Luke was expected. Nobody had been sick in it yet, and claiming to be queasy was a good enough trick to get you out of almost anything.

He picked away slowly at his Oats-You-Like. He couldn't afford to finish it because his mother would just swipe the bowl away and shove it in the dishwasher. If only Dad and Molly and Luke would just *go*! Then Mum would probably fall asleep on the spot and he could sneak away with the oats *and* the scrambled egg. Every minute he was wasting down here, the dragon's strength was draining away. It was probably crying for him at this very moment, crying for food. It was agonising just thinking about it.

But Molly, oblivious as ever to the currents of atmosphere around her, was still happily counting out chocolate eggs. Everything was perfectly fine and dandy on Planet Multicoloured EggHunt, in the far-off galaxy where Molly made her home.

'I found four eggs,' she said happily. 'Two of mauve and two of pink.' So Molly had found the egg in the bathroom, the one Josh had hidden for his mother. This didn't come as a great surprise. 'I love how you can tell who hid them! It's the best game ever. How many have you found, Josh?'

Josh hadn't found any. Nor had his mother, and Josh would have bet that she hadn't hidden any either.

'I found two yellow,' said Dad, and Molly beamed with delight. 'You're in second place and Josh and Mum are equal last.'

Josh ate another mouthful of oatmeal, and said nothing, and prayed for them to hurry up and leave.

9

Eventually Molly and Dad and Luke set off on their drive and Mum, as predicted, muttered straightaway that she was going upstairs for a lie down and faded into nothingness like a ghost.

And so Josh was easily able to sneak miniature helpings of oatmeal and scrambled egg up to the dragon, but by then the food had set, hard and cold and solid. The dragon was curled up listlessly in a corner of the ice cream tub, and though it perked up briefly at the sight of the food – or maybe it was the smell – this didn't do any good, because it had no teeth and couldn't chew. It tried to swallow a mouthful of egg, and immediately began to gag and choke, and by the time it had coughed all the egg back up it was even emptier and hungrier than before, and Josh could tell from the rasping noise that its throat hurt. It gazed up at Josh with a pitiful and bewildered look that stabbed him to the heart.

Josh had never known a feeling like it. Nothing had ever depended on him in his whole life. His mother was allergic to animal hair, so they'd never had any pets. It was such a huge leap, from being responsible for nothing, to having a living creature think you were its mother and look to you for food. He wasn't equipped for it! Suddenly he felt a pang of longing for his own mother. If only he could go to her and get help! The whole crushing weight would be lifted off his shoulders. But even as the thought popped into his mind, he knew that it was out of the question. His mother was going through almost exactly the same thing herself, ten times over, with Luke. Luke was the boundary of her world now. She had no energy left for anything more.

The dragon slumped into a doze on Josh's duvet, in a fold which must have seemed like a valley surrounded by fluffy duvet mountain ranges. Josh made a half-hearted start on the job of sorting out the mess on his floor. At least it was something to do. It was better than sitting and gazing at the dragon, watching as it gradually shrank with starvation. Soon he had uncovered a clear area of carpet, revealing the stain marks the dragon had left where it first spilled out of its egg. Josh fetched a cloth and scrubbed them clean. The dragon slept on. Probably it was slipping into a coma and that would be exactly what Josh deserved. During the night he'd had ideas of constructing a play area for the dragon on the carpet, where it could run around and exercise without getting lost. He could have built it out of Lego, and perhaps with a bit of thought and planning he might even have been able to work out how to construct a climbing frame and a slide. A sandpit! He somehow knew that this dragon would love a sandpit! It could dig around and bury itself for fun, and when it learned to start making flame – which was, after all, the basic *reason* for being a dragon – the sand would extinguish the fire before it could take hold. A practice flamethrowing area! What dragon could possibly hope for more?

But all that seemed now like a distant dream.

Josh flopped down on the bed alongside the dragon, which barely even twitched an eyelid. Its strength was fading by the minute. Josh had to *think*. To think calmly and logically. What type of animal was closest to a dragon? Almost certainly a lizard. They had legs and scales and hatched from eggs. Maybe some of them could even fly. So, what did newborn lizards eat? Josh was certain this was the right question, but he hadn't the slightest idea how to find the answer. Newborn birds – which also hatched from eggs and could *definitely* fly – well, Josh was almost certain they started off eating things their mother had already swallowed, started to digest and brought back up again. He'd seen it on TV, a whole nestful of gaping baby beaks squirming and stretching and squealing for their share, and the mother bird basically *vomiting* food she'd eaten earlier, squirting it from her own beak into their hungry mouths.

He had no doubt that his mother would do exactly the same for Luke if she thought it would help him. This was how you could tell a proper mother. All the normal rules of what was disgusting and revolting simply didn't count. Josh just wasn't good enough.

'But I don't even have a beak, and you're not a bird anyway!' he said, helplessly, for all the world as if the dragon had been begging him to try. It was crazy, talking to a dragon, but the whole world had tilted dangerously on its axis and *become* crazy, and in any case Josh needed to talk and there was nobody else he could talk to.

The dragon half opened its eyes and said *cheeeeep*.

And in the same second, before Josh had a chance to react, his bedroom door flew open and Molly burst in, saying: 'Who was that? Who was that saying "I'm hungry" just now?'

'NO!' screamed Josh, but it was too late. Molly had seen.

'Ohhhh!' She clapped a hand over her mouth, stood and stared. 'Oh! What is it? It's adorable! Why didn't you say? Where did you get it from? Hell*ooo*!' This last 'hello' was addressed in something midway between a coo and a squeal to the dragon, which looked up.

Josh gave a wail of agony. 'Shut the door!' he hissed. Molly was frozen to the spot, gazing at the dragon. 'I said *shut the door*!' Molly glided over to the bed as if in a trance, holding out her hand. The dragon no longer had sufficient energy to climb up, but it rested its chin on Molly's thumb and began, gently, almost hopefully, to lick it.

Josh slammed the door shut. The dragon and Molly both jumped, and turned to look at him with four huge reproachful eyes. 'Molly,' he said urgently. 'You have to promise not to tell. You have to promise! Mum and Dad can't know.'

'Why not?' asked Molly, only half listening. She was still making cooing noises. The dragon seemed, very faintly, to be cooing back.

'They wouldn't understand!'

'Oh, OK,' said Molly, although Josh knew for sure that if anyone had tried to fob him off with such a pathetic explanation he'd have had a million questions to ask. Like – *what* wouldn't they understand? Josh didn't understand himself! And here was Molly nodding peacefully as if she understood everything perfectly. Probably in Molly's universe the arrival of a dragon wasn't anything particularly remarkable. A person who talks to a space cucumber and believes their bedroom to be haunted by a night ghost train called Clumbermould clearly lives by different rules.

The dragon, who hadn't given Josh a single glance since the arrival of Molly, went *chirrup chirrup cheep*, and Molly said: 'But Josh, she's hungry! Why haven't you been feeding her?'

'*I've been trying!*' Josh almost screamed. 'And what do you mean, she? Why would you think it would be a girl?'

'I just know,' Molly said with quiet confidence. 'She's called Sabine.'

Everything was being taken out of his hands. 'What d'you mean, you know? What kind of a dumb name is that?'

'It's her name.' Molly had picked the dragon up and was blowing softly against its nostrils. The dragon blew back. Josh clenched his fists in agony. It was his dragon! It wasn't supposed to do that with just anybody! Especially not Molly!

And yet – Molly seemed to be able to communicate with it in a way he, Josh, couldn't. 'I was going to call it Firestorm,' he said, though if he were brutally honest he had to admit that the name had never fitted and that he had never actually begun to use it. He'd assumed the dragon would be a boy because in all the books he'd ever read and all the films he'd seen, everything that wasn't human always was! It was the rule! Everyone knew it. From the seven dwarves via Baloo the Bear to Casper the Ghost, from every single hobbit to E.T. the extra-terrestrial, from the Genie in Aladdin to R2D2 the android, from Tom and Jerry to Bugs Bunny, not to mention Woody Woodpecker and the Pink Panther, from Buzz Lightyear to Scooby Doo, if a thing wasn't human it was a *boy*. It was the same in computer games: Lara Croft was allowed to be a girl because she was human, but Crash Bandicoot? Sonic the Hedgehog? Boys. Girls were already so strange that if you let them be not-human as well as strange the universe would probably explode. That was how things worked, and messing around with rules like that was very dangerous. It was tampering with nature.

But: 'She's a she,' said Molly, and Josh was forced to admit to himself that the dragon looked nothing whatsoever like a Firestorm. It looked like a Sabine. *She* looked like a Sabine. Whatever a Sabine was.

'So if you're such an expert on dragons,' he said sharply, 'then what does she want to eat? Because she's very nearly starving!'

'Where did you get her from?'

'From the Internet,' Josh said, trying to find words to explain the inexplicable. 'She was supposed to be a virtual pet.' Molly looked blank. 'A pet that just lived on the computer. And somehow she became real.' His heart did a cartwheel as he put this into words for the very first time. Anyone listening would think he had gone completely insane.

Anyone except his sister Molly. In Molly's world anything could happen and often did, and so almost nothing could surprise her. For as long as he could remember Josh had been annoyed and frustrated by his sister, but now, for the first time ever, he found himself feeling deeply grateful that she was exactly as she was.

'The Internet on the computer?' Molly asked.

'Yes.'

Molly frowned. 'So how did she get here?'

'Molly, she was in that egg! The big blue one with the purple spots!'

Light began to dawn in Molly's face as pieces of the puzzle clicked into place. 'Ohhhhh! Right! I told you I didn't paint that egg!' she added. 'But you wouldn't believe me.'

Josh winced at the memory. Of course he hadn't believed her. He had been one hundred per cent sure he was right, and he'd turned out to be completely wrong. It was a deeply unpleasant sensation. 'I'm sorry,' he said awkwardly. 'I really thought . . . I mean . . . '

But Molly wasn't paying attention. 'Well, if she was living in an egg then perhaps we should give her egg to eat. The egg must have been feeding her before she was born.'

This was strikingly logical. 'She did try to eat the scrambled egg I brought her this morning,' Josh said. 'But it was too hard.'

'We need a raw egg,' Molly said. 'I bet that would feed her.'

'We ate all the eggs up for breakfast!'

'There might be some left. Let's go and see.' Molly had been cradling the dragon tenderly. 'Sabine, we have to leave you for a while.'

'Her home's down here,' Josh said, reaching down behind the bed and pulling out the ice cream tub. It looked small and shabby and distinctly inadequate, but Molly said nothing, just laid Sabine down on the bedding and made a chirruping noise of goodbye.

'Molly – wait. Who's downstairs? Where is everybody? I don't hear Luke. Why are you back anyway? I thought you were going to the lakes.' He wouldn't have been so careless otherwise. He hadn't expected them back for hours.

'We decided we wouldn't go without you. We just drove round to the bypass and back. Luke fell straight-away asleep, but as soon as we got home he started crying. Didn't you hear?' Josh shook his head. 'So now Mummy's taken him for another drive over to visit Grandma Helen.'

'And Dad?'

'Doing his work on the computer.'

'All right, then. Come on.'

There was precisely one egg remaining in the fridge. Josh took it and cracked it into a cup. If anyone noticed it was gone, well, he could just say he'd broken it by accident.

'I think it's the yolk that's the nourishing bit,' he said. 'Let's try that on its own first. Can you fetch a spoon?' It felt good, just for a moment, to be the one in control. He managed, with some difficulty, to extract the yolk and to tip it into a second cup, leaving most of the colourless eggwhite behind.

'That's good,' said Molly, nodding. 'I think she'll like that.'

'But she won't be able to eat it,' Josh said, remembering the dragon's earlier feeding disasters. 'She'll climb into it and it'll go everywhere. And we've only got one! She needs a bottle, like Luke has. Molly – do you have anything like that? For your dolls? A tiny bottle?' It sounded like such a promising idea, but Molly just shook her head.

'My dolls are grown,' she said. For a few moments they looked at each other blankly. And then: 'But I know what we can use! The squeezy thing for my ears!'

'The *what*?'

'When I had my ear medicine, remember? It had a tiny squeezy thing for squeezing the medicine into my ear.'

Josh thought she had slipped back into nonsense talk, but then suddenly his brain went *click*.

'Ear drops? You had ear drops?'

'I had a bad ear! You don't even remember?' said Molly, sounding quite offended.

Josh didn't, not really, but it seemed tactless to say so. 'Oh, *that* bad ear. Molly, do you know what happened to the bottle? Did you finish it all up?'

'No,' said Molly. 'It's in the cupboard in the bathroom.'

The dropper was attached to the inside of the cap, and it looked perfect for the job. Josh filled it up with water and emptied it again six times, to get all the ear medicine out – it was quite probably poisonous – and then, scarcely daring to breathe, he stabbed it into the egg yolk, sucked up a whole dropper full, coaxed Sabine's jaws open, put the dropper in and squeezed.

It all seemed to go down. Maybe the force had sent it shooting straight down to her stomach.

'She likes it!' Molly said with a long breathy sigh of relief. 'She ate it all up!'

Josh thought it was a bit too soon to be cheering. 'She may be sick yet,' he said. 'She was always sick before.'

'No,' Molly said, with the same calm confidence that she'd been showing ever since she first set eyes on the dragon. 'This is good. It's going to be all right.'

'Shall I give her another lot, do you think?' It went against Josh's nature to ask Molly for advice, but he couldn't help himself. She *knew*.

'Just one more,' Molly said. 'Then keep the rest for dinner.'

Sabine opened her mouth wide all by herself when she saw the second helping coming, and this one went straight down as well.

It was almost impossible that anything could be working so fast, but to Josh's eyes the dragon looked stronger already. Her eyes, which had taken on a dull, cloudy look, were beginning, very faintly, to sparkle. Life was visibly flowing back into her.

Molly bounced on the bed with sheer delight. 'She's getting better! We saved her! We did it!'

But a dark voice in Josh's head was whispering

silently: 'Not *we*. *You* did it.' And before he knew it he had said the words aloud.

'Don't be silly,' Molly said. 'We did it together!' And Josh knew that in Molly's place he would never have been so generous. He would have claimed all the credit and told her she was stupid and that she knew absolutely nothing about anything. It was just habit. He'd been talking to her that way all her life. Was Molly a nicer person than he was? It wasn't a pleasant thought. And now the dragon had turned to Molly and was moving towards her, making its way towards her hand to be picked up, even though Josh was the one who'd given it the miracle feed. And he knew in his heart of hearts that it was fair, and that he ought to be pleased for her, but the truth was he felt plain jealous.

10

The atmosphere at breakfast the next day was heavy with anxiety, secrets and unspoken thoughts. Nobody was paying much attention to the food.

Luke, unbelievably, was still crying, a low-key whimpering that every few minutes grew to a full-blown howl. On and on it went. Josh had learned more or less to filter it out when Luke was in another part of the house. This sounded unfeeling, but really it was such an irritating sound, and Josh couldn't actually do anything to help, so what was there to be gained from listening? When Luke was in the same room, however, there was no ignoring it.

Why, oh why, do babies make such an especially horrible noise? Josh's class had been studying natural selection, and so he knew that this was the reason for almost everything human beings have become. Perhaps the babies whose crying sounded the most unbearable had a better chance of survival, because people just gave them whatever they wanted, right away, to shut them up. If you had twin babies and not enough food to go around, then naturally you would feed the one that made the worst row. *That* made sense. But, on the other hand, weren't those very same babies more likely to get killed? You only had to shake a baby just a little bit and it could die. It was an interesting question but it was one you couldn't ask, not unless you wanted to be rounded up and taken to a child psychologist, like Ryan Downing, who didn't ask questions about murdering babies but who still wet his bed.

'I just don't understand it,' Josh's mother was saying for the third or fourth time. 'Three hours we were at my mother's, three whole hours, and not a peep out of him the whole time!'

'Well, isn't that a good thing?' asked Dad, who was trying in vain to persuade Luke to take some milk.

'But as soon as I got back here with him it started up again! Almost the second I walked in the door! How do you think I feel, when my mother can soothe him and I can't? He's better with anyone than he is with me!'

'Lin, you know that's not true,' Dad said wearily, though in fact Josh had noticed that in general Luke *was* calmer when being held by his father than by his mother.

Mum was on the verge of tears, he could tell, and as if reacting to the atmosphere the baby was suddenly sick all down Dad's shirt front.

'Shall I take him for a while?' Josh asked, but: 'I can manage my own baby, thank you very much!' his mother said, almost angrily, snatching up Luke who immediately let out a terrible screech of distress. 'See?' she said to Dad. 'Do you see what I'm saying? The moment I touch him he begins to scream twice as badly.'

'I think he's just reacting to the tension he's feeling from you, Lin,' said their father. 'If you could only . . .'

'So you *are* saying it's my fault!' their mother cried, and rushed from the room with Luke, who was now screaming at full blast.

‘I didn’t say that . . . ’ their father began, but it was too late. He sat forward and buried his head in his hands. Josh squirmed with discomfort. There was nothing in the world worse than your parents having a scene like that in front of you, as if you weren’t there. Whenever something like this happened – and recently it had been happening more and more – Josh always felt somehow guilty, as if he’d been the one to set it off. This time it was probably his fault for thinking a thought about babies being shaken to death, with their own baby crying right there in front of them. It was wicked of him. You can’t always help what you think, and of course he hadn’t meant Luke, he hadn’t meant any particular baby, it had been a *general* thought, but it had brought darkness and discord trailing in its wake and straightaway things had begun to get worse.

And his mother’s behaviour was starting to seem slightly crazy, which was frightening.

Dad raised his head. ‘Anyway,’ he said. ‘Molly. I haven’t heard a single word out of you all morning. How’s the egg hunt coming along?’

Molly and Josh exchanged glances. They had already decided that the hunt must be called off. The last thing they wanted was for their parents to be poking around in their bedrooms, looking for hiding places or for eggs.

Molly said: ‘I think we should stop doing the egg hunt until Luke’s better.’

‘There’s no need for that . . . ’ her father began, but Josh chipped in and said Molly was right, nobody felt much like egg hunting at the moment.

‘I don’t want you two to feel you can’t enjoy yourselves in your own home!’ Dad said.

‘Don’t worry,’ Molly said with a mysterious smile. ‘We’re enjoying ourselves lots.’

‘Are you?’ It sounded as if he didn’t quite believe it.

‘And another thing,’ said Josh. ‘Molly and I are going to make our beds every single day from now on, and keep our rooms tidy, and put all our dirty clothes in the laundry, so Mum needn’t worry about any of that at all. We started already this morning.’

‘Oh, Josh.’ Dad looked really touched. ‘That’s so good of you. You’re such thoughtful, helpful children. I’m really proud.’

Josh smiled faintly, but the compliments had a bitter taste, because of course the reason for volunteering for this extra work wasn’t to help Mum and Dad at all. Just like the postponement of the egg hunt, it was meant to keep their parents out of their rooms as much as possible. His father was giving them such a warm affectionate look, and they didn’t deserve it in the slightest. Josh felt so ashamed he wished he could disappear, but there was nothing for it but to smile back.

It was really only Molly’s room that they needed to keep secure, because Sabine had moved in with her now, and Josh had been helpless to prevent it.

They had been settling the dragon down to rest in the ice cream tub when all at once Molly clapped her hand over her mouth and said: ‘I have an idea!’ Josh said nothing, almost as if he could derail the idea by not asking. He felt somehow certain both that it would be an outstandingly good idea and that it would leave him feeling worse. 'Sabine should come and live in my doll's house,' Molly said, glowing with delight at the brilliance and rightness of this.

Five minutes later all three of them were next door in Molly's room, where Sabine had already been introduced to her new home. Josh could see already that it was going to be perfect. Molly's doll's house was huge. It had a tall red roof and a hinged front that lifted right up. At a stroke, Sabine's living accommodation had improved from an ice cream tub to a luxurious five-room detached residence. Already Molly had filled the bath, put fresh cotton wool down in the bedroom, removed all the dolls except for one (who was called Patti Peachtree, and who was allowed to stay in case Sabine got lonely) and was busy working out the dragon's toilet arrangements.

And Sabine, after trying without success to figure out how to climb her staircase, had settled down in an armchair in the living room, apparently to watch television.

Josh surveyed this cosy scene with glumness. At this rate their dragon, supposedly a flamethrowing mighty mythical flying beast, would soon be conditioned to a life of idle domestic comfort. It could only be a matter of time before Molly installed a swimming pool and a jacuzzi. It was all deeply wrong. It went against nature. Maybe – if only – the dragon had been a boy, as it should have been, then he would have felt able to put his foot down about its upbringing. As it was he had been reduced to a helpless bystander in a girls' doll's-house world.

And that wasn't the only thing bothering him.

'Molly.'

'Mmm?' Molly was humming happily to herself as she rearranged the living room furniture.

'It's going to be a bit awkward moving this to my room. I mean – a doll's house!'

'You want it in your room?'

'Yes! I mean, no! I mean – but she was mine first!' Wasn't it obvious what he meant?

'Everyone's going to notice if we do that,' Molly said, and Josh knew she was right. In Molly's room the doll's house was more or less invisible. It was where it was supposed to be. Transfer it to Josh's room and it would stick out a mile. Mum might not be very alert these days but there were some things even she couldn't help spotting.

'But – if we leave her in here – what's going to happen if she needs something in the night?'

'Well, I'll take care of her,' Molly said, and even as she said it Josh realised the stupidity of his objection. Of course Molly would take care of her. Molly had already proved herself a thousand times better at doing that than Josh was himself.

'Lazy girl!' Molly said now to Sabine, who was still reclining in the armchair in that full dozy state that can follow on from a good meal. 'You have to practise the stairs!' She lifted Sabine to the bottom of the staircase and clicked her fingers at the top. The dragon made another attempt at climbing, this time managing to scramble to the third stair before slithering back down and landing thump on her bottom.

'Good!' said Molly. Sabine shook her head, dazed, and then waddled out of the doll's house onto the wide open space of Molly's bedroom carpet. Already she was much steadier on her feet.

'Careful!' squeaked Josh. 'Don't let her out!'

'Why? She can't get out of the door.' They had propped the bedroom door open with a shoe, to make sure they would hear any approaching footsteps and not be taken by surprise.

'She might run off! She might hide under the wardrobe! We couldn't move the wardrobe. Even both of us together couldn't move it an inch.' It was good to learn there were some things Molly hadn't thought of.

But:

'Sabine!' called Molly, making a sound that was half chirrup and half whistle, and holding out her hand invitingly. The dragon, who had been investigating Molly's left slipper, turned on the spot and made her way straight to Molly, climbing up onto the outstretched hand and lifting her head up expectantly for praise.

'She comes when she's called,' Molly said, stroking the dragon contentedly.

'Molly.' There was a question Josh had been putting off, because he was almost afraid to know the answer.

'Yes?'

'When you first heard her – when you were outside my room and you heard her and you came in. You said you'd heard a voice saying "I'm hungry". Do you remember?'

'Of course I remember.' Molly placed the dragon back at the bottom of the stairs. 'Sabine, you have to learn to do this or you won't be able to use the whole of your house. Now try again.'

'Molly. You know the noises she makes. She doesn't talk. Why did you think she was saying she was hungry?'

Molly sat up and considered this, apparently for the first time.

'I just heard what she meant,' she said at last.

'But that's not possible! She just makes cheeping noises! Are you saying you heard something different?'

'No,' said Molly. 'I heard the cheeping and at the same time I knew what it meant.'

'But don't you even think that's *odd*? I mean, weren't you surprised?'

'I didn't think about it till just now,' Molly said, shrugging. Josh gave up. He understood more or less what she was describing. It was the same sort of thing as, say, when a person spoke perfect French. If that person heard a French person talking, they would hear exactly the same as Josh would hear, but at the exact same instant the English translation would pop into their head, without their even having to think about it. Whereas to Josh the same noise would just sound like gobbledygook, unless they said 'bonjour' or 'au revoir' which was all the French he knew.

None of this explained why Molly should be fluent in Flagondra while he, Josh, didn't understand a word.

Perhaps if you spent all your free time conversing with toys and dolls you began to pick up non-existent languages. Perhaps Flagondra was very similar to Space-Cucumberese. Whatever the explanation, it left Josh more excluded than ever. He was starting to get used to it.

11

Molly had not been able to provide any solution to the long-term feeding problem, and – at last! – Josh was able to come up with a useful suggestion of his own. Right back at the very beginning, when he was sitting at the computer choosing the Flagondra egg, he'd been told that while he was waiting for it to hatch he should be studying and making plans for the newborn's care. And like an idiot he'd thought *boring!* and taken no notice whatsoever.

So surely it would tell you on the Technomon web site how to feed a Flagondra?

They couldn't get near the computer all Saturday evening, because Dad worked and worked right through until after they'd gone to bed. So after breakfast on Sunday, that dismal breakfast with Luke crying and Mum storming off all upset, Josh said to his father:

'Would it be OK for me and Molly to have the computer for a while?' and Dad said yes, that was fine, he was just going to sit quietly for a few minutes and then tidy up the kitchen. He looked miserable and tired, and Josh wished he knew a way to make things better. He wasn't used to his father acting this way. He was usually so lively, so full of fun and jokes. It made Josh feel awkward and uneasy, as if there were a stranger present in his father's skin.

He and Molly fled to the computer room, and Josh took the mouse. It was time to revisit Technopolis.

Welcome to Technopolis!
The greatest virtual pet centre on the Internet!
Raise your own Technomon!
More than six million owners already!

'Woooo!' said Molly, dazzled, and pressing close up to Josh to watch. He could feel her warm breath on his cheek. 'This is amazing! Can I play?'

'It's not really a *game* right now, Molly,' Josh said, clicking on **Your Pet**. Up flashed the following:

Congratulations!
It's a girl!!

Type: Flagondra
Name: [ ]
Weight: 24 g
Height: 66 mm
Level: 1
Owner: Shadow Demon
Owner No: 6,666,666

Under the words 'It's a girl!!' was a picture of Sabine, looking straight at the camera with what Josh was coming to recognise as her characteristic, eyes wide open, eager-to-please expression.

‘Wow!’ said Molly. ‘Sabine’s on the computer! That’s amazing!’

‘Molly. That’s where she’s *supposed* to be!’ said Josh. ‘It’s her being *here* that’s amazing.’

Molly leaned further forward, scanning the words closely. She was a good reader for her age, the best in her class, but she couldn’t quite manage this.

‘What’s a Fl . . . a Flag . . . ’

‘Flagondra. It’s the type of pet. They’ve got lots of others. I chose a Flagondra because I thought it sounded the most fun.’

‘But Sabine’s a dragon!’

‘I think a Flagondra is a breed of dragon,’ said Josh. ‘Like a Yorkshire Terrier is a breed of dog.’

Molly nodded, satisfied. ‘And why does it say all those sixes?’

‘It must mean . . . ’ Josh thought for a few moments, running through the words in his head till they sounded right. ‘. . . I was the six million six hundred and sixty-sixth thousandth six hundred and sixty-sixth person to join Technomon.’ *More than six million owners already*, he remembered. So he had acquired this remarkable number just by a chance of timing. Was that what made Sabine . . . different?

‘You need to put her name in,’ Molly said, and Josh typed ‘Sabine’ into the empty box. ‘Good!’

‘But this page isn’t helping us find out what she eats,’ Josh said. ‘I’ll have a look around.’ He clicked back to the front page and straightaway spotted a button called **Caring for your Pet**.

‘This’ll be it!’ he said. A new screen opened up, listing all the Technomon by type. He’d never realised there were so many! Dolphix, Pengoridon, Sprattler and Emeranth, Camelope, Wolvermoth, Cluckhopper and Sparkanoid . . .

Molly gasped. ‘What’s all of these names?’

‘They’re all the different types of Technomon you can have,’ Josh said, and straightaway realised that ‘you can have’ had been a poor choice of words, for Molly squealed with excitement and said: ‘Can I have one? A Fl . . . Fl . . . Flitbugler? Or – no – let me have a Forkfoot! *Please*? I’ll take such good care of it? Please, Josh?’

‘Molly, don’t be ridiculous! We can’t even take care of the pet we already have!’ Josh clicked firmly on ‘Flagondra’, and a new page loaded with buttons labelled **Illness and Disease**, **Exercise**, **Education**, **Training**, and – wonderful sight – **Food**. The answer to all their problems was just a click away! He hovered with the mouse pointer over **Food**.

‘Go on!’ breathed Molly.

Josh clicked, and up came a screen with the most beautiful title he could imagine:

Feeding your Flagondra

Yes!!!

‘Read it out loud,’ Molly urged, and Josh read:

‘The newborn Flagondra should be fed on a diet of Pentacorn milk and the sap of the TangBang tree. When it reaches a weight of 40g it is ready to move on to a diet of moonbeam smoothies, spangleberry purée, gourmet snowballs and rainbow cream pie. At a weight of approximately 60g . . . '

Josh's voice tailed away. He couldn't quite see himself and Molly knocking up these exotic dishes in the kitchen.

'I don't know what any of those are,' said Molly.

'They'll be things that only exist in Technopolis,' Josh said.

'So can we get them from there?'

'I don't know!' He clicked on 'Pentacorn', and an explanation popped up:

Pentacorn. A five-horned quadruped, once plentiful in the Scorched Forest but now almost extinct, due to the devastation of their habitat by fire, and also to the high frequency of tragic fatal stabbings within the herd.

He clicked on 'TangBang tree':

TangBang tree. This tree is an extraordinary sight, its spiral trunk forming a natural helter skelter for young forest Technomon such as Squirulina and Chipsqueak. However, the relentless series of forest fires caused by the local Flagondra population has reduced this once widespread tree to a fraction of its former numbers, mostly located in the very south of the Forest, near the Marmolean Plain.

This was just brilliant. The Flagondra had accidentally flamed to death all of their natural food supply. Now what were Josh and Molly to do?

‘I really want a Chipsqueak!’ Molly sighed, dreamily. Josh looked sternly at her. ‘Sorry,’ she said. ‘So, can you go and catch a Pentacorn? Please?’

‘Oh, yeah, right! Just like that! Even if I knew how, they’re almost extinct!’ Probably you needed to be a level 18 magic user, possess an enchanted amulet and a snakeskin lasso and be in charge of an entire herd of Luponio even to get near to catching a Pentacorn. You’d need a map. And you’d need . . .

And then Molly had one of her startlingly simple ideas.

‘We should ask the shopkeeper for help,’ she said.

‘What shopkeeper?’

Molly waved at the computer. ‘The shopkeeper of this pet shop.’

‘But it isn’t a pet shop! Haven’t you been paying attention at all? It’s . . . ’ and then Josh’s voice faded as he realised that it didn’t greatly matter *what* it was. Of course they should ask for help. Why on earth hadn’t he thought of that himself?

‘There’s a message board,’ he said, clicking around till he found it. ‘I’ll leave a message and just hope somebody answers it.’

‘*Good* idea,’ said Molly, twisting a piece of hair into braids.

Josh typed in the following message:

To: *anyone*
From: *Shadow Demon*
Please could you tell me where I can find a Pentacorn or a TangBang tree? It’s an emergency. Thank you.

He clicked **Send**, before Molly could spot the name *Shadow Demon*, which had sounded quite cool at the time, but which looked somehow ridiculous with his sister breathing down his neck.

'So what do we do now?'

'We wait,' Josh said. 'We'll go up and see Sabine and you can clean out her home,' he added, not entirely kindly. 'Housework. She'll need her water and her bed changing, and all the furniture should be dusted every day.' If Molly was taking over Sabine she could take over all the boring stuff as well. But Molly just said, 'Oh yes! Good idea!' as if dragon housekeeping was simply the most fun in the world, and scampered off upstairs.

They let Sabine out to explore while Molly took care of the house. She rushed straight over to say hello to Josh and to have her ears tickled, then disappeared under the bed. Josh wanted to try whistling and calling her like Molly did, but he was afraid to try in case the dragon took no notice. That would be so humiliating. He'd have a go sometime when Molly wasn't around.

'We've used an awful lot of cotton wool,' Molly said, fluffing up Sabine's clean bed. 'Mum might ask where it's gone.'

'Just say you took it to put in your Easter baskets,' said Josh. It was amazing how quickly you learned to be a creative liar.

'I'll fetch some proper bedding from school tomorrow,' Molly said.

'How are you going to do *that*?'

'I'll clean out our hamster.' Another problem solved,

just like that. Who would ever have thought Molly would turn out to be so *capable*?

And then Sabine emerged from under the bed, batting a marble with her front legs.

'Molly. Look!'

Molly turned and gave a gasp of adoration. The dragon advanced, dribbling the marble along in front of her with an expression of glee.

Their dragon was playing football.

Instantly she skyrocketed in Josh's estimation. 'Good girl!' He jumped up. 'Molly, give us some goalposts. Furniture!'

Molly handed over a couple of dining room chairs and Josh lined them up about a foot away from the dragon. 'Now, you go girl! Go for goal!'

Sabine caught on straightaway. 'Yes!' Josh yelled. 'All on her own down the right wing, taking on one defender, two defenders, she aims for the top right hand corner of the net – and she scores! Flagondra United 1, Rest of Technopolis nil!'

Molly was on her feet dancing with excitement. 'Do it again!'

Josh plucked the ball from between the dragon's legs and placed it back in the centre. Sabine raced over to it in something midway between a trot and a canter, and immediately set off again for goal.

'Two nil!'

'Three nil!'

'Four nil!'

Five minutes later it was sixteen nil and Sabine had

collapsed with exhaustion. Molly picked her up tenderly and placed her on her bed. *Cheep*, said Sabine, and this time even Josh could tell that she was hungry. She'd had nothing to eat yet today.

'Let's see if somebody answered our message,' Molly said, and they closed the front of Sabine's house and headed back downstairs.

There was a message waiting for them.

To: *Shadow Demon*
From: *Minerva*
My incredible magical powers tell me that you are a newbie with a newly hatched Flagondra to feed. Don't worry, you don't have to go chasing wild Pentacorn. Sometimes life can be much simpler than it seems. Just go to the shops and buy what you need. Good luck!

'Shops? What shops? I never saw a shop that sold Pentacorn milk or thingy tree sap!'

'Not real shops,' Josh said, clicking away furiously. 'Technopolis shops. This place is absolutely full of shops. Look! Shopping Mall! It was right there on the front page!'

'But we haven't got any money,' said Molly.

'Yes we have!' Josh said. 'When I started off it said if I hatched an egg I'd get 500 Technickels. And I haven't spent a single one because I didn't even think of it till now. We're rich, Molly. Let's go shopping.'

12

The Technopolis Shopping Mall was vast. *Frockbusters*, *Gadgeteria*, *Morgana's Apothecary*, *Sparklet's Jewels*, Josh read. *Bank of Luetta*, *Technopolis Tourist Board*, *Toys! Toys! Toys!*, *Poems and Potions*. There were specialist Technomon shops: *Tedrapodium*, *Dolphix Accessories*, *Cluckhopper World*. And – wonderful sight – an entire Food Court devoted to establishments selling food and drinks of every imaginable type. *Cheezebox*, *Tooty Fruity*, *Smellicatessen* and *Cakehole*; *Monster Cookies*, *Killer Cereals*, *Chocoland* and *Beachburgers*. Best of all, tucked away between *Juicy Lucy* and *Salad Days*: *Rambeau's Baby Foods*.

Yes!

Josh clicked on the shop, which opened up to reveal a dazzling amount of stock. There must have been at least eighty different types of food and drink. The drinks came ready-to-use, in feeding bottles (wow!!! how useful was *that*???) and the food mostly in little glass jars.

'May I help you?' asked the shopkeeper, who was a sheep – a sheep wearing spectacles, and with a fetching purple quiff, but a sheep nonetheless.

'Well!' said Molly. 'Why would a shop have a sheep running it?'

'Maybe it's Woolworth's,' said Josh, and Molly screeched with laughter. It was very gratifying. He thought for a few moments, and then added: 'And I bet if there's a chemist shop it's run by a cat!'

'Why?'

'Puss in Boots!' Josh said, almost helpless with giggles, and this time Molly laughed so much she slipped off the side of her chair and ended up in a pile on the floor.

'Josh!' she said when eventually she was able to speak. 'That's so f... f... funny!' And she was off again, rolling about with mirth.

Josh glowed. He hadn't shared a moment like this with anybody for such a long time. Not since Claudio had gone back to Italy. Three whole months. Who would have thought that the next time he broke someone up with laughter it would be his *sister*? He'd never even noticed that she'd grown old enough to understand a proper joke.

He realised with a slight jolt that he hadn't thought once about Claudio in the whole of the past three days.

The sap of the TangBang tree cost 9 Technickels a bottle and it was a pale, watery yellow. The Pentacorn milk, slightly more expensive at 11 Technickels, was – pink. *Bright* pink.

'It looks like strawberry milkshake,' Molly said, scrambling back onto her chair. 'Go on, then – buy one!'

Josh clicked on **Buy**.

'How many of this item would you like to buy?' asked the sheep, and 'Get two!' said Molly. 'And two of the TangBang thing. That should be enough feeds for today. What does 11 TN mean?'

'It's the price. Eleven Technickels. Technickels are the money they use here.' Josh typed in '2', and 'Thank you for your custom,' said the sheep, bowing.

Josh repeated the whole process for the TangBang tree sap. 'An excellent choice!' the sheep said. 'And now, could I interest you in our very own freshly-made pistachio snowballs? Packed with all the vitamins a growing Technomon needs, they melt on the tongue...'

Josh escaped before the sheep could persuade him into a rash purchase he knew he would regret later.

'Now let's go to the toyshop,' said Molly.

'Molly, no. We don't need...'

'Oh, go on, Josh! Don't be such a spoilsport! Just one little toy! She's just a baby. She needs things to play with.'

'*One* toy, then,' Josh said, clicking his way into *Toys! Toys! Toys!* where the shopkeeper was a green and yellow caterpillar. 'Just one!'

'Can I choose? Please?' asked Molly.

'Well – all right. But it has to be something quite cheap. Our money won't last forever.' I'm going to have to find out how to get more money, Josh thought. Milk and sap cost very little, so there was no immediate urgency, but all the same...

Molly was gazing spellbound at the contents of the toyshop. There was practically nothing you couldn't buy to amuse your Technomon. An entire section was devoted to soft toys. There were model railways, remote-controlled cars, footballs, yoyos, pogo sticks, skateboards and glowstars. All tastes and budgets were catered for.

Molly dived straight into Soft Toys. 'This is what she needs,' she said firmly. 'A cuddly toy to take to bed with her. Something to love when we aren't there.'

'Oh, *Molly*.' Josh winced. 'That's so soppy.' For minutes on end Molly had been acting almost human, and then with no warning she'd turn back into a girl.

'Well, we're going to be out at school for hours! Here – this is what I want.' Molly pointed to a teddy bear. A turquoise teddy bear.

Josh instinctively shrank from this notion. 'Molly. It's just a soft toy! It won't do anything! It's boring. And it's – it's *turquoise*,' he added. Somehow it wouldn't have been quite so tasteless a purchase had it been any kind of proper bear colour. But:

'You promised I could choose! You promised!' Molly's voice was rising with an insistent tone of distress.

'All right, all right!' At 27 Technickels the turquoise teddy was at least one of the cheaper items in the shop. At the other end of the scale, they had motor go-karts that cost 2250 TN! How ever long would it take to save enough money to buy a go-kart? For a moment Josh imagined Sabine steering her very own go-kart around Molly's room, her face lit up with delight. If only they could afford it! He wanted his Technomon to have the very best of everything! It was so frustrating to be poor.

The go-kart might be nothing but a distant dream, but perhaps they could afford just *one* more small toy right now. Josh slid the mouse pointer around the shop, finally settling in a section called Battle Toys. Now here was the thing! Swords, sabres and shields, lasers . . . this was just what a young dragon needed! 'I'll get her a starsword,' he said, half to himself. The starsword was a slightly reckless purchase at 38 TN, but it would be well worth it . . .

'*You said I could choose!*' Molly shrieked, right in Josh's ear.

'You don't have to deafen me!'

'*But you said!*' She looked close to tears.

'You can have the bear! OK? I'm going to get the starsword *as well.*'

'You said just one toy. And she won't want a starsword,' said Molly. Josh took no notice. The starsword lit up with shooting stars that flashed and shimmered the entire length of its blade. How could anybody not want it? He ordered one turquoise teddy and one starsword.

'Can I interest you in a set of holographic juggling balls?' asked the caterpillar. 'This brand new line is bound to be massively popular and will sell out fast. Buy now or risk missing out!'

Molly's eyes lit up, and Josh backed out of the shop hastily.

'Sabine would be a *good* juggler,' Molly said. 'But never mind. Where do we get our stuff from?'

Josh paused. He hadn't quite thought the shopping process through to the goods collection point. 'I don't exactly know,' he said. They looked at each other, blankly.

'They are going to give us the stuff?' Molly said uncertainly.

'You don't think we're supposed to feed the computer Sabine with computer milk?' Josh's heart sagged with disappointment as this idea occurred to him for the first time.

'But that's no fun at all! I want the stuff! I want it for real!' Molly's face was crumpling up with misery.

Josh said: 'Let's think about this. How did they get the real Sabine to us here?'

'How'm I supposed to know that? I didn't even see her till after she was born!'

'But Molly – you saw her first. You were the one who found the egg. Remember?'

'Of course I remember. But . . . '

'So where was it when you found it? Exactly where? Try and concentrate.'

'But I know that already. I told you, only you wouldn't listen. It was sitting right on top of that picture, on the floor.'

Why would a picture be on the floor? 'Molly, you're not making sense. What did this picture look like?

'It was all different colours. There were birds flying in the sky, and there was a mountain, and the egg was sitting right on the top of the mountain.'

'You mean the mousemat?'

'I didn't notice a mouse. There was a pony, and . . . '

'No, no – Molly, a *mousemat*! Like this! A thing you slide a computer mouse over!'

'Oh, right. Yes, it could have been one of those.'

'It was the Technomon mousemat!' This had to be a key element to the solution. 'So – where's it gone?'

'I don't know,' said Molly.

'Well, when did you see it last?'

'When I found the egg,' Molly said. Josh groaned in despair. What had hc done with the thing? He could remember throwing it onto the floor in a fit of temper, and then nothing.

'Molly, we have to find it!'

Molly turned her head and looked round the room. 'But it could be anywhere,' she said. 'It might even have been thrown out with the rubbish!'

Josh buried his head in his hands with frustration.

'The rubbish people don't come till Monday,' Molly said. 'When's Monday?'

'Tomorrow.' Josh brightened. 'And you know – Mum would never have bothered picking up a mousemat. I don't think she's even been in here for weeks. If I haven't moved it and you haven't moved it . . . '

'. . . it has to be Daddy!'

Their father was putting the finishing touches to his tidy-up of the kitchen. Luke could be faintly heard crying upstairs.

'Yes, of course I remember that mousemat,' he said. 'How could anyone ever forget it? It was so bright I was afraid to look directly at it. I picked it up from the floor and put it in one of the drawers in the computer desk.'

'Thanks, Dad!'

'Does anyone fancy a trip out today? I was thinking we might go swimming, or maybe the cinema . . . '

'Later, all right, Dad? I mean . . . ' as his father's face

fell '. . . just right this minute me and Molly are right in the middle of something.'

'Oh, OK then,' his father said, but Josh still felt guilty.

He searched desperately for something friendly to say. 'Erm – nice kitchen, Dad! Good job!' His father gave him a quizzical look; Josh fled.

Molly had already found the mousemat. 'It's so pretty!' she said, tracing her finger along the course of the river. 'What do we do now?'

'I guess we wait,' said Josh. 'Put it down flat.' Molly placed the mousemat carefully on top of the computer desk. They waited. Nothing happened.

'Perhaps it won't do it while we're watching,' said Josh. 'Let's go and play with Sabine for a few minutes and then come back and check.'

'But what if Dad came in and found a . . . Josh! Josh! *Look*!'

Something was happening. It was hard for Josh to find the words to describe it because he had never seen anything like it before. There was a – a disturbance in the air directly above the mat, a swirling and crackling, almost as if there were about to be a thunderstorm. He found his eyes averted, pulled away to the side despite his will, and then there was a tiny flash of light, the atmosphere relaxed into proper indoor air, and when Josh looked back there was, lying on top of the mountain right in the middle of the mousemat, a miniature, perfectly-sewn, turquoise teddy bear.

There was a silence, as both Josh and Molly drank in the dizzying fact that they could click on anything they wanted in all of the dozens of shops in Technopolis, and turn a computer picture into an actual thing. In a weird sort of way, it was even more fantastic than having the dragon, because the dragon had just arrived, without their knowledge or control. Now they'd learned the system, and they could have anything. Anything they wanted.

Molly picked up the bear very gently with the tips of her thumb and forefinger. 'It's perfect,' she said. 'Look.' The bear had tiny green glass eyes, and was sewn together with microscopically small stitches. They sat together, speechless, admiring it.

'I'm going to call him Sheringham,' Molly said at length.

'Huh?'

'Teddy Sheringham. It's such a nice name. I heard it on the television.'

'Molly, *no*! You can't! Teddy Sheringham's not a bear. He's a footballer.'

'Well, that's perfect then, because so is Sabine. Let's go up and show her.'

'But . . . ' They both looked down at the mousemat. Nothing was happening. No storms, no hurricanes, no shimmering of the air. But something might happen at any moment. They were owed four bottles and a starsword. 'We'll take it with us,' said Josh. They went up to Molly's room and set the mousemat down carefully in a quiet corner, and almost at once there was a hazy shivering, and again Josh found himself looking away, and this time when he looked back two bottles had arrived, one of TangBang sap and one of Pentacorn milk.

‘Can I feed her first?’ Josh asked – asking Molly’s permission! – and Molly said yes, he could, and Josh chose the pink Pentacorn milk, because it looked so much richer and more nourishing, and Sabine was very hungry – they knew that from the *cheeps* coming from inside the doll’s house.

The bottle was a perfect miniature replica of one of Luke’s; plastic, with a rubber teat, and it even had tiny markings up the side, hairline thin. Molly lifted the front of the house and the dragon came running out straightaway, squeaking, begging for food. Could she smell the milk? Josh lifted her into the palm of his left hand and held the bottle to her mouth. Sabine began, contentedly, blissfully, to suck. Finally, after two days, she was getting her first proper feed of dragon food in a proper dragon bottle.

Molly watched, beaming. ‘Everything’s going to be all right now.’

‘Mmm,’ said Josh, who didn’t quite believe it.

‘Isn’t it funny how the air around Sabine sort of shakes? Just like it does on the mat when they send us something?’

‘Huh?’ Josh knew what she meant about the air shaking above the mat, but as far as he could tell the air around Sabine was perfectly still.

‘Never mind,’ said Molly. ‘Look! She’s finished it all up.’

Sabine had drained every drop. She stretched her limbs with satisfaction, sending a featherlight flutter through her wings, stepped to the edge of Josh’s hand and peered over.

‘She wants to go down,’ Molly said.

‘I know that!’ Josh said, placing the dragon on the carpet. She scampered off immediately under the bed, returning seconds later with the marble.

‘She wants to play football again! We should have bought her the goalposts in the toyshop.’

‘She’ll be fine with the chairs,’ Josh said. He’d seen the goalposts himself, *and* their price. They were outrageously expensive, a ripoff, a trap for over-indulgent Technoparents. Josh hadn’t even considered buying them. Well – not for more than half a minute.

There followed another lengthy session of football. Sabine was as adorable as ever, and her enthusiasm for the game was charming to behold, but after a further twenty goals Josh found himself starting to feel ever so slightly bored.

‘You know what she reminds me of?’ he said.

‘What?’ Molly seemed to have endless patience with the dragon.

‘You. When you were about two years old. You’d want to play the same thing over again and again and again. Everyone else would get bored with it but you never did. And Sabine’s just the same!’ He replaced the ball in the centre circle for Sabine’s twenty-second run for goal. ‘It’s like she’s turning into a toddler already.’

‘Maybe one day of dragon time is the same as one year of our time,’ said Molly.

Josh thought about this. At one day old, Sabine had been able to walk fairly well but she couldn’t run. At two days she could do a semi-run with a football, and steer it reliably into a very wide goal without anyone tackling her.

Maybe one year to one day wasn't so very far out. In which case she should probably be finished with bottles and onto the next stage of food already.

'If that's right, then in two or three weeks she'll be fully grown,' he said, trying to imagine how big Sabine might be by then. It seemed very unlikely that the doll's house would still be enough to contain her. And then he thought of all the things a fully grown dragon would do, like flying and breathing fire, and all at once it seemed that their problems, far from being solved, might have only just begun.

13

Luke had cried for almost the whole of the weekend and he was still crying on Monday morning. He must have been totally exhausted but it didn't make the slightest difference. Mum, sitting at the breakfast table in her dressing gown, was ashen, great dark smudges like bruises sunk beneath her eyes.

'He's lost weight!' she said, for the fifth or sixth time. 'Can't you tell?' The spectre of the hospital hovered in the air like a stormcloud.

'Well, you're going to phone the doctor's surgery as soon as they open at eight thirty,' Dad said soothingly (and also for the fifth or sixth time). 'I'm sure they'll see him straightaway.'

'And what if they say I should have taken him to the hospital at the weekend? I would have done – but for all those hours at my mother's he seemed perfectly all right. I thought he was better! How was I to know?'

'You weren't to know, Lin. I'm sure nobody's going to blame you.'

'How can you be *sure*?'

Josh groaned silently. This conversation had been going round in circles for at least ten minutes, and whatever Dad said, it was never the right thing and it never helped. But of course he couldn't just sit there saying nothing because that wouldn't have been right either. His father was starting to look almost as washed out as his mother.

Sabine, in cruel contrast to Luke, was thriving. Josh and Molly had both risen early, Molly to water and exercise Sabine, and Josh to order the day's feeding supplies from *Rambeau's Baby Foods*, where the sheep had welcomed him like an old friend and tried to sell him a blender. He had checked the **Your Pet** page, only to find that Sabine had gained 4 grams since the day before, while her height had gone up by 3 millimetres. It was clearly all a matter of finding the right food.

'Perhaps you're not feeding Luke the right stuff,' he said without thinking. 'Maybe that milk isn't . . . '

He could tell he'd made a bad mistake straightaway. His mother stiffened and snapped: 'Are you telling me I don't know how to feed a baby?' in a tone of real fury.

And suddenly Josh had had enough, enough of this whole Luke thing that dragged on and on forever and was turning his mother into a waking nightmare. He stood up, pushed his chair back and half-said, half-shouted: 'That's not fair! I never said that! Any time I try to help, you just shout at me and pretend I said something I didn't!'

He had never spoken to his mother like this in his life before. In fact he had probably never spoken to *anybody* like this. The whole room froze. Molly's eyes, huge as saucers, darted around from person to person.

Josh's father got up and said: 'I think it's time to get you two on your way to school.' Josh and Molly slid out behind him into the hall without a backward glance.

Josh was half expecting to get the telling off of his life. 'Dad,' he said. 'I didn't mean . . .'

'I know you didn't, old man.'

'I just thought that maybe the milk Luke's drinking doesn't suit him. That's all!'

'I know. And actually, it's a really intelligent idea. Maybe he's allergic to that brand of milk. I hadn't thought of that. But listen, Josh – your mother, she's not herself just now.' Josh said nothing. Did Dad think they hadn't *noticed*? 'She's so very worried and tired,' his father went on. 'I was up half the night myself but I couldn't get her to go and lie down. It's just the same as when she was at the hospital. No matter what anyone says to her, she won't leave him for a moment. I think she's afraid that if she takes her eyes off him . . . that . . . well, anyway.'

There was an uncomfortable silence.

Eventually Molly, who hadn't spoken a word since she came down to breakfast, said: 'Dad. Luke is going to be all right, isn't he?'

Their father put a hand on her shoulder. 'I think so, Molly. He's come through so much. This is his first real setback for a long time. And it's probably just a bug, something any baby might get. Or as Josh said, perhaps he's allergic to something. Don't worry. OK?'

'Mmmm – OK,' Molly said, but she didn't sound convinced.

'Your mother's going to see the doctor this morning and I'm sure that'll make all the difference. Now – I'll get home as early as I can, but it may not be until after five. OK?'

'OK,' said Josh, reluctantly. It was going to be horrible, arriving home to a house with just Mum and Luke in it. If only his father would take the day off! 'Are you sure you have to go to work?' he asked, not with any great hope. 'You don't look very well.' This was true.

'Josh, I have no choice,' his father said, walking with them to the gate. 'I've been wondering – perhaps I should ask Grandma Helen to come and stay for a while. She's been offering for months, ever since . . . '

'No!' Josh said. Surely things hadn't got this bad? All the time Luke and Mum had been in the hospital Grandma Helen had wanted to move in and take care of Josh and Molly and Dad, and Dad had quite rightly said thank you very much but no, they could take care of themselves, and they *had* taken care of themselves. Grandma Helen wasn't a bad person but she did have a way of taking over. She would move all your things to different places without telling you, which wasn't really right when they weren't her things and it wasn't her house. And although Josh had never seen Dad and Grandma Helen be anything other than perfectly polite to each other, he had a feeling that they weren't exactly comfortable together.

And now, after they'd come so far, Dad was thinking of changing his mind and asking her to stay.

'There wouldn't be anywhere for her to sleep,' Molly said firmly.

'We could work something out. She could share with you, Molly . . . '

'No!' Josh and Molly said together.

‘There’s no need, Dad, honestly,’ Josh added, contemplating this disastrous scenario with some desperation. ‘We’ll be fine. Haven’t we always been fine? We’ll take care of Mum when we get home. Honestly we will! Trust us!’

‘OK.’ Their father’s face crinkled into something that was almost, though not quite, his usual grin. He gave them both a hug, and they set off for school.

‘Grandma Helen would find Sabine straightaway,’ Molly said with a small shiver.

‘I know!’ Josh’s stomach lurched at the thought. It had been hard enough leaving Sabine alone in the house as it was. They’d given serious thought to hiding her in the garden shed. The shed was tucked away at the end of the garden and there wasn’t the remotest chance of Mum going out there. It was a big shed, but it contained a variety of very strange things, left by the people who’d lived in the house before the Harpers. Mum and Dad had meant to clear it out for years, but whenever they’d been in a sufficiently energetic mood there had always been something that needed clearing much more urgently. And so the Harpers had simply added more and more stuff to the stuff that was there already.

Molly and Josh went down to have a look.

‘Dad always says there’s everything here but the kitchen sink,’ Josh said.

‘That’s here too!’ Molly said, pointing to the far corner where there was, indeed, an ancient porcelain sink, perched on top of a pile of mouldy encyclopedias. A birdcage hung from the ceiling. There was a small refrigerator without a door, a bulky filing cabinet, an old-fashioned record player, and, stacked against the right-hand wall, a pile of what appeared to be cannonballs.

'We *could* leave Sabine here,' Molly said without enthusiasm. 'We could carry her house down.'

'Carry her house here and back every day? How long do you think it would take until somebody saw us?'

'You mean Mum and Dad?'

'Anybody! What about the neighbours?' Josh waved an arm vaguely in the direction of the houses on either side.

'Do you think they'd tell?'

'They might get nosy and come and look! Wouldn't you, if you saw two kids carrying a doll's house down to a shed every morning before school and collecting it afterwards? Molly, we can't leave her here. This shed doesn't even lock. Anyone could get in. There might be burglars!'

Molly nodded. There was no question about it – Sabine would have to stay indoors. They planned it carefully. The doll's house was turned to face the wall, so there was no chance of Mum catching sight of Sabine through a window. It wasn't a very exciting view for the dragon, but they were hoping she would sleep most of the day. She'd had half an hour of vigorous early morning exercise followed by a thick bottle of pink Pentacorn milk to settle her down. And she was very active during the night. Josh was starting to suspect that she was nocturnal.

But even so it would be impossible to relax for a

second until they could get back home to check on her.

Josh walked into the classroom feeling six inches taller than the Josh who had left it on Friday. School had always been such a big thing in his life. But, compared to owning a baby dragon, it was *nothing*. It just didn't seem important any more, and as school shrank, so by some magical process did Josh himself seem to grow.

Of course, the fact that Shane Walters and Dylan Brasher weren't back also helped. It would have been wonderful to think they might be gone for good, but Josh knew better. They'd been suspended before, both singly and together, and they always returned a few days later. The school had a policy of never excluding anybody permanently – a policy of which it was very proud, though Josh couldn't see why, because the system seemed to benefit nobody at all. Dylan and Shane knew they could get away with murder. Whatever they did, they were always given another chance. The normal kids, the ones who just wanted to get on with their lives in peace, knew their tormentors would soon be back, as did the teachers. And as for Shane and Dylan, they never learned a thing in school anyway, and would quite certainly be far happier slumped at home in front of the telly pigging out on crisps and chocolate biscuits. But no, they were always allowed back and so everyone carried on being miserable.

William Beresford was back in his seat, all by himself as usual, wearing a shiny new pair of glasses. For a moment Josh, the new, improved Josh, thought about going over to speak to him. It seemed as though somebody should. But even in Shane and Dylan's absence, people were still wary of William Beresford. It wasn't just that they were scared of being done over during break if they were seen talking to him. There was actually something quite scary about William himself. He was different. Perhaps it was a side effect of being so clever, but he never really seemed to act like a kid. He was like a grown-up trapped in a child's body, and somehow he had created an invisible barricade around him that nobody cared to cross. He wouldn't want to talk to me anyway, Josh thought, quite relieved to have come to this conclusion, and slipped into his seat behind Carrie and Bethany.

'Hello, Josh!' they said, turning round to greet him. 'Did you have a good weekend?'

'Oh, just the usual,' Josh said. 'Boring really. You know . . . you know that Techothing you were telling me about?'

'Technomon?'

'Did you go and try it?'

'I knew you'd like it! Did you get a pet?'

'No! My sister did,' Josh said. He had planned the conversation up to this point.

'Oh, your little sister? I know her, she's in the Infants? She's so cute.' Josh pulled a face. 'What kind of Technomon has she got?'

'A Flag – Flag something. I think it's some kind of dragon.'

'A Flagondra!' they both cooed, in perfect unison. 'They're adorable!' Bethany said. 'That would definitely have been my second choice.'

It wasn't easy to find the right words to phrase his next question.

'Can you – these Technomon – they're just something on the computer, right?' Bethany and Carrie looked blank. 'I mean – you wouldn't be able to get one in real life.' Even as the words came out he was regretting them. It wasn't possible that other people's Technomon had come to life. He'd *know*. Or – well – would he know? Josh wasn't about to tell anybody, so why would anybody tell him? Perhaps there were thousands of Technomon really living in the world, and none of their owners dared to say a word.

But that couldn't happen. So many secrets could never be kept. He didn't have to look further than his own classroom to know that. Carrie Lindwell and Bethany Marks wouldn't have been able to keep such a thing quiet for five minutes. And now they'd think he was completely insane. Why hadn't he kept his mouth shut?

But no – not at all.

'Not in this country you can't get them in real life,' Carrie said. 'Only in America. It's so mean!'

'*What*? Get what? How?' Josh blinked in mystification. Whatever response he had been expecting, it certainly hadn't been this.

'Technobeanies!' they chorused.

'You *what*?'

'Oh, Josh! You know. Like Beanie babies. You must have heard of Beanie babies!'

'Oh, right.' Of course he'd heard of them. Molly had dozens of the things. Each one came with labels telling you its name (they were all called things like Fizz and Smudge, Bippety and Boppety, Binky and Stinky) and its birthday. For a while the entire Harper family had been expected to celebrate the birthday of some small bear or rabbit or bird at teatime practically every week. It had been sickening. Josh opened his mouth to say this, but found it closing, the words unspoken. He wasn't going to trash Molly to these girls. Last week he would have done so without a second's hesitation. But Molly had been pretty good over the weekend. There had been moments when he'd almost felt pleased to have her for his sister. She was his ally now. They were sharing something extraordinary, and he felt bound to her by a new loyalty.

'Well,' said Carrie, 'Technobeanies are just the same except they never released them over here.'

'It's so unfair!' trilled Bethany.

'Did you want one for your sister's birthday?'

Josh nodded, although Molly had only just had a birthday, three weeks ago.

'They've just made a limited edition purple and gold Flagondra, as well,' sighed Bethany. 'It would have been perfect!'

Josh was saved from answering by the arrival of Miss Hollis, but in truth he'd stopped listening. Carrie and Bethany had nothing useful to tell him – how had he ever thought they could? Nobody in the whole world could. It was becoming ever clearer that he and Molly were in this alone.

14

Josh and Molly walked home so slowly that at times they seemed to be walking backwards. The dragon, they were sure, had not been found. If that had happened the ripples from the fallout would have reached them already. So uppermost on their minds was a distinct dread of getting home to find their baby brother still screaming, and their mother talking in Greek and eating the wallpaper.

They didn't discuss these things. They didn't need to. They just knew.

Both of them had had a difficult day at school. It was hard to pay attention in class. This had hit Josh worse than Molly, because in the Infants school nobody really expected you to have learned to pay proper attention yet. But Molly had actually fallen asleep after lunch, which was frowned on even in the laid-back world of the Infants.

When Josh pushed open the front door he heard female voices talking. He found his mother sitting in the kitchen with Luke and a woman called Wendy, who was something to do with the hospital and who had visited almost every day when Luke first came home. Wendy was plump and hearty with shiny skin and aggressively large white teeth, and Josh had never liked her much, but right now he couldn't have been more pleased to see her.

He could tell at a glance that his mother, though still drained and tired, had somehow relaxed.

'Well, hello there, young man!' said Wendy. Molly had sensibly disappeared upstairs.

'Hello,' Josh said abruptly. 'So what's wrong with our baby? Did someone find out?' Luke was in his carrycot, crying.

'We had him in today for a thorough check,' Wendy said. 'And although we'd like to see him putting more weight on, we're pretty pleased with his progress on the whole.'

'And he didn't cry the whole time we were there,' Mum said, giving Luke an almost resentful glance, as if to say, 'How could you let me down like that?'

'Isn't it always the way?' said Wendy. 'Just like when you book a dentist's appointment, and the moment you get there the toothache goes away!'

Josh wasn't interested in Wendy's teeth, which had basically annoyed him since day one. 'He's crying now,' he said.

'We think we know what the problem is,' said Wendy. 'We think he's got colic.'

'What's that?'

'It's a kind of tummy ache that babies get. It's not uncommon at all. It's very distressing but they do get over it eventually.'

Eventually?

'How long is eventually?' he asked, and, 'Oh, sometimes it can take months!' said Wendy. Josh's mother gave a tight little smile.

'*Months?*' Josh tried, and failed, to imagine months of this – Luke crying day and night, his mother sleepless and unpredictable in her anger and her moods, the whole family disintegrating. But his mother just said:

'At least we know what's wrong with him now!' and she and Wendy began nodding at each other in a very united, knowing sort of way, making it clear that Josh had completely missed the point.

Over the next few days the Harper household gradually settled into a new routine. For Luke and Mum it was a complete reversal of their previous existence, huddled up indoors safe from germs and all the badness of the world. Once it was discovered that the only thing to reliably cheer Luke up was to be taken out, his life was transformed into a social carnival. Mum packed him into the car and took him all over. Luke went out to lunch every day of the week. He paid extended visits to Grandma Helen, he went for long drives in the country and was taken for leisurely walks in the park. All at once the house was full of shopping, for a trip to the supermarket would get Luke out of the house and buy a couple of hours of peace. The cupboards bulged with food, and, because Mum's memory was not terribly reliable, several items were bought three days in a row. Multipacks of toilet paper in four different colours appeared in the bathroom, making trips there a new and hazardous experience.

Then, after he got home from work, Dad would bundle Luke back into his car seat and take him for yet another outing. Often, rather than sitting down to eat at home to a backdrop of screams, the whole family went out for dinner. It was worth the cost, Dad said, to enjoy a peaceful meal, with the baby sucking contentedly on a bottle. Everywhere they went, waitresses would go all gooey at the sight of him. 'Ahhh! He's so tiny! Look at those little hands!' Sometimes even the customers at the next table came over for a look and a drool.

It was the strangest thing, but in many ways Luke's illness had *improved* things for the family. Mum had needed to start getting out and about, and now she'd been prodded into doing so, you could tell just by looking at her that she was better for it. The walks in the fresh air had put some colour back into her cheeks. Needing to find places to take Luke, she'd got back in touch with all her friends, the friends she'd forgotten about the day Luke was born and never thought of since. She'd even made a new friend, somebody called Caitlin who had a baby almost as small as Luke. They'd met in the park and now they hung out together drinking coffee and talking baby talk.

Luke still cried all through the night, but now Mum had a diagnosis she was prepared to take turns at sleeping, rather than guarding the baby every single second. Dad bought earplugs. Neither of Josh's parents was getting enough sleep, but at least Mum wasn't going mental any more, and the tense, fraught atmosphere around her had almost disappeared.

And of course, the fact that the house was so often empty was highly convenient for Josh and Molly. It made it much less likely that Sabine would be discovered.

Sabine was flourishing. Her Technomon record showed that she had shot up to Level 4, and she was gaining weight so fast Josh sometimes swore he could actually see her growing as she sat in his hand, just as you sometimes think you see the minute hand move on a clock. She had progressed to a diet of moonbeam smoothies, spangleberry purée and gourmet snowballs. Sabine loved gourmet snowballs with a passion, and her squeaks of joy when they bought her her favourite flavour, frosted double choc chip fudge, were so enchanting that they let her have one almost every day despite the price, a hefty 14 Technickels. How could they refuse?

Their dragon's personality was turning out to be entirely frivolous. All she wanted to do was play. 'We have to get her more toys!' Molly said, and, 'We can't afford more toys!' Josh would answer, knowing that he really ought to sit down at the computer and figure out what they were going to do about the Technopolis money problem. The trouble was that as their Technickels drained away and the problem became more and more urgent, the vastness of it seemed so overwhelming that Josh was increasingly unable to do anything about it, because he was afraid to try.

Rather to his annoyance, the dragon had become deeply attached to her turquoise teddy bear, Sheringham. Sabine wouldn't settle down to sleep, in her brand new nest lined with hamster bedding, unless the bear was there with her, and there had once been an awful panic when the bear – who was, after all, very small – was lost for some hours, eventually being found stuck to the sole of Molly's slipper.

Even more irritating was the fact that the starsword had been a total flop. Sabine was quite clever with her front legs, but she had feet, not hands, and feet were not designed for gripping starswords. She would sit up on her hind legs and grip the sword, and she always seemed delighted by the flashing lights, but it was awkward for her, and Josh suspected that if she weren't so keen to please him she would never bother with it at all. And he'd spent 38 Technickels on the starsword!

'It's not meant for Flagondra,' Molly said. 'Toys that you have to hold are meant for Technomon that have hands, like a Boboloon or something.'

'A what?'

'A Boboloon. It's a sort of really big monkey.'

'How do you know that?'

'I looked. I know all the names of the Technomon now.'

'You looked? How did you do that? You don't even know the password!'

'Yes I do,' Molly said. 'I watched your fingers typing it and I remembered it.'

'Molly! That's very bad of you! You should never spy on another person's password.' But Josh couldn't really blame her. When you were Molly's age people were always trying to keep things from you for one reason or another, and you had to use all the ingenuity at your disposal just to keep up. He knew that in her position he would have tried to do the same himself. But he didn't have anything like such a good memory as Molly's, and by the time he had a chance to use the password himself he'd have probably forgotten it. Molly never forgot anything, ever.

'If you've been messing around on the Technomon website, you might at least have tried to earn some Technickels,' he grumbled, which was horrendously unfair when he'd made no effort to do so himself.

'I did,' said Molly, setting out the obstacles for Sabine's daily football workout. Sabine *loved* football. By now she was so skilled at running with the ball that they had to fix her up a slalom course to negotiate before she shot for goal. Josh had even been persuaded to buy her a proper football. The football – 28 precious Technickels' worth – had arrived on the mousemat in the usual fashion. Josh had been expecting some nasty plastic rubbish, but no – it was a beautiful ball, black and white panels perfectly stitched. It was, he had to admit, infinitely better than the marble, which didn't even bounce. Sabine had started to practise headers and to learn Keepy-Uppy, and was already much better than Josh at both.

'You did?' Josh picked up the dragon, who was quivering with excitement at the sight of Molly's preparations. 'You earned us some money?'

'I wasn't good enough,' Molly said. 'I tried some games. They have all these games where you can win Technickels if you get a good score. But I was rubbish.

There was this one game where you had to fly a helicopter into a mouth and down through the human body without crashing it. I couldn't score more than 11 points, and you needed 50 to start winning money. I never even made it as far as the stomach. I kept crashing into the back of the throat. Then there was a game like ten pin bowling only you had to roll apples to knock over bottles. I was a bit better at that but I still lost.'

Josh's spirits rose at this news. He was quite good at computer games. Perhaps making money wasn't going to be so difficult after all. He'd give it a go tomorrow evening.

15

The next day, Josh's class went on an outing to the Globe Theatre to learn how plays had been staged in Shakespearian times. The class was united in their complete lack of interest in this topic, and the general boredom led to considerable disruption. Shane and Dylan were back, nastier than ever and twice as ugly. Their gang snaffled the back seat of the coach and spent the journey belching, jeering, punching each other, punching other people, spitting, pulling faces and making obscene gestures out of the back window, and encouraging Alex Burkett, who was famously prone to travel sickness, to vomit into the hair of the people directly in front, who were of course William Beresford and Josh, forced to share a seat as the only unmatched pair in the class.

William Beresford had his head buried in a book and seemed to be able to shut them out of his consciousness, though Josh couldn't tell if this was real or just an act. Can anybody *really* fail to notice a boy hanging over the seat behind, having his back thumped by two other boys to a chorus of 'Spew, spew, spew shampoo, cures split ends and dandruff too, stinks like snot and sticks like glue'? It didn't seem likely.

School trips had been something to look forward to, when Claudio had been there. Claudio never took any nonsense from Shane and Co. Claudio would have jerked his head upwards and smashed it into Alex Burkett's jaw, trapping his tongue, which was flopping out in the ready-to-retch position, between his teeth, drawing screams of agony and pints of blood, and putting an end to matters. But of course they knew that, and so they'd always left Claudio alone.

At the Globe Theatre Shane and Dylan were soon raging and charging around shrieking: 'Oh, Juliet! Get thy knickers off!' 'Go on, Romeo, give her one!' 'Romeo's gay!' and Miss Hollis was asked to remove them, which meant that the other teacher who'd come on the trip had to take them to a café, and after they met up later people started complaining that they'd much rather have gone to a café than to the Globe Theatre and it just wasn't fair. They themselves would have insisted that Romeo was gay, if they'd known there was going to be a *reward* for it. Miss Hollis lost her temper and started yelling, and people stopped and stared, and Shane Walters and Dylan Brasher, who always considered it a great victory to get a teacher to scream, gloated and smirked and punched the air, while swallowing the final crumbs of their giant-size chocolate muffins.

Then, on the way back, the coach got stuck in a three-mile tailback on the motorway. They didn't arrive home until half past five, a full hour late, and for Josh the journey was pure torture. Not only did he have to endure the kicking and thumping of his seat from behind, accompanied by baying and screeching and an endless torrent of filthy abuse, but as the time dragged on and on he was feeling increasingly uneasy about what might be happening at home. He was beginning to wonder if he had ever actually been able to relax for a single second since the dragon had arrived. Whenever he was out of the house half of his mind stayed behind.

He was right to have worried.

As soon as he got home he flung his bag onto the floor, raced upstairs and burst into Molly's room, to be faced with the astonishing sight of their dragon coolly executing a hundred and eighty degree turn on a jet black skateboard decorated with flashes of red and gold, at the very top of a high curving ramp. Scattered around on the carpet was a pile of other toys. A Slinky. A set of holographic juggling balls. A bubble machine, a set of football goalposts and a little green remote controlled car. It was like Christmas morning. Molly was clapping her hands with delight.

Josh slammed the door shut. 'What's this? What do you think you've been doing? Don't tell me you bought all these at *Toys! Toys! Toys!*'

Molly stuck her lip out. 'You said you'd start earning money from the games today. And Sabine needed toys! She . . .'

'How much money is there left?' Molly said nothing. 'You've spent it all, haven't you? How could you? What if I'm rubbish at the games? She'll starve to death! Did you even bother to get her a smoothie for her tea? I thought not!' Josh felt close to tears. After the awful day he'd had, this was just too much to take. 'Molly, you're completely irresponsible! And you forgot about Rule Number One: always keep the door open so we can hear people on the landing. That could have been Mum or Dad coming in just now, not me. And... and you shouldn't let Sabine go skateboarding without a helmet!' he added, hysterically. 'It's dangerous!'

As if to emphasise the point, the dragon lost her balance and fell off the skateboard, rolling over and getting to her feet without any apparent harm.

'Now she's upset!' Molly said, lifting up Sabine to comfort her. The dragon was making distressed little whimpering noises. 'She hates it when people shout. It frightens her.'

'Oh right! So it's all my fault! You're the one who...'

But, in the heat of the moment, Josh had forgotten Rule Number One himself. Suddenly, the door, which he had banged behind him in his fury, opened wide and their father stood in the threshold. Josh's voice tailed away to nothing, and Molly gave a squeal of panic, for Sabine was sitting there in her hand, fully visible and still making the whimpering sounds. There was no time to hide her. It was over.

'Is everything all right up here?' Josh's father asked. 'There's been a lot of banging and shouting going on.'

Josh and Molly sat frozen in silence.

Dad's forehead wrinkled in puzzlement. 'Hello?'

Josh didn't know where to look. His eyes were drawn toward Sabine and Molly, but he resisted the urge. He couldn't look his father in the eye. He hung his head and stared at the floor, and waited helplessly for whatever it was that was going to happen.

Molly recovered her senses first. 'Everything's fine,' she said uncertainly. 'We just – had an argument.'

'Just an argument? I've never seen Josh look so guilty. Have you broken something? Josh?'

Josh forced himself to look up. Sabine had stopped whimpering and was making excited little squealing sounds instead. It was simply not possible to ignore her.

But his father was paying no attention to Sabine at all. He was looking down at Josh.

'We haven't broken anything,' Josh said. 'We were arguing about a game.' He had never sounded less convincing in his life. His father said, 'Hmmm . . . ' and, casting a final suspicious look back over his shoulder, he left the room.

It felt as if Josh and Molly had been holding their breath for five minutes.

'He didn't even notice Sabine!' Molly said.

How was that possible? 'He must have thought she was a toy,' Josh said. 'I mean – look at all this.' He waved his arm at the loot all over the floor. 'Nothing but toys.'

'But she was making a noise the whole time!'

They looked at each other.

'Perhaps he thought she was a squeaking toy.' It was true that Sabine looked more like a toy dragon than a real one. She had that Disneylike, brightly coloured, cute appearance that was typical of Technomon. She looked like a *cartoon* dragon.

'What was she saying?' Josh asked.

'She was saying hello. She was really pleased to see him. She wanted to be friends.'

'That's so like Sabine. She's always going to think everyone wants to be her friend,' said Josh, who was far from sure that this would be the case.

Molly nodded. 'Well, we're the only two people she's ever met. Why wouldn't she think that? She's all surprised and sad now that he didn't take any notice of her.' Sabine was, indeed, looking noticeably crestfallen. 'You know what I think?' Molly went on. 'I don't think he *could* hear her.'

'Dad's not deaf. Of course he could hear.'

Molly shrugged. 'Well, that's what I think.' She set Sabine down on the carpet and pressed a button on the bubble machine. A stream of bubbles flew out, shimmering and twinkling in the light. Sabine gave a gasp of delight and set about chasing them, her troubles apparently forgotten just like that.

Josh sighed, sat down on the floor and rested his head on his knees. 'I'm sorry I shouted at you.'

'It's OK. Josh?'

'Yep?'

'Tell me again why it is that we're keeping Sabine a secret from Mum and Dad?'

Clearly, 'Because they wouldn't understand' wasn't going to be a good enough answer this time.

'Because I don't know what they'd do,' he said. It was the plain truth. What did grown-ups do when faced with the impossible? Josh's parents were both in their thirties. They'd lived three times as long as he had with their beliefs about the world, and so for them the shock would probably be three times worse. 'It's not as if it's a – a baby squirrel that we've got here, Molly. It's not a real creature. This is a dragon.'

'How d'you mean, not a real creature?'

'Molly, you know that dragons don't really exist. Well – except for her.' He nodded at Sabine, bounding about blissfully popping bubbles.

Molly frowned. 'They don't? But they must do. I've seen pictures.'

'Molly, you've seen drawings and you've seen computer-designed dragons. In films and in video games. But you've never seen a photograph, have you?'

'I thought I had,' Molly said.

Josh shook his head. Only a few weeks ago he'd have torn into his sister for being so stupid. He'd always been really mean to her for believing in things that weren't real. But the truth was – though he wouldn't dream of admitting it – that since Sabine's arrival he hadn't been so certain about anything any more, and he had actually been researching dragons himself, just to be entirely sure. 'There aren't any dragons, Molly. Only Komodo dragons, and they aren't dragons at all. They haven't got wings and they don't breathe fire. They're just a kind of gigantic lizard.'

There was a pause while Molly took this in.

'There weren't even dragons long ago and they all died?'

'Became extinct, you mean? Like dinosaurs? No. Never.' He couldn't blame Molly for not knowing this. At her age he hadn't been much wiser. He'd known about the obvious things, like Father Christmas – as soon as you start nursery school there's some smart-mouthed kid just bursting to tell everyone Santa isn't real. But in so many cases the issue of reality never seems to arise: witches, goblins, zombies, trolls. Nobody tells you. You just have to work it out as you go along. Josh had been at least nine before he'd realised that he would never meet a unicorn.

'So I think they'd take her away. We wouldn't be allowed to keep her here. And after that I don't know what would happen to her. But probably she'd end up with scientists. They'd want to do experiments on her. And you know what Sabine's like! She'd trust them, she'd think they were her friends and that they were going to bring her new toys to play with, and then they'd hurt her!'

Molly's eyes were welling up with tears and her face had paled with shock, so Josh quickly added: 'But that's not going to happen!' He didn't want to give his sister nightmares. She was getting little enough sleep already.

He stood up. 'I'll go and log in to Technopolis and try and win some money on the games, OK? Don't worry, Molly. I'm sure we'll manage just fine.' He had no idea if this was true, but it sounded like the right thing to say.

Molly gulped. 'OK,' she said. 'But I still don't think Dad could hear Sabine. And I don't think he could see her either,' she added, but Josh had already left the room.

16

It took Josh an hour and forty minutes to earn enough Technickels to buy Sabine food for the next twenty-four hours. Some of this was his own fault for being lured into the Lucky Star Casino, where 50 of his hard-earned TN promptly disappeared into the hungry jaws of the slot machines. So he had to go back and earn them all over again.

The problem with the games at Technopolis was that it took ages and ages to rack up a good score. Josh played a game called Planetary Pool for over half an hour, completing fourteen levels, only to be awarded a measly 22 TN. You couldn't buy one rainbow cream pie with that!

'I'm not going to be able to keep this up,' he said to Molly. 'I'd have to spend more than an hour every night playing. And even that would only be enough for food. No more toys. Some nights Dad needs the computer anyway.'

'If I were you I'd ask that Minerva to help you,' said Molly. 'She was really nice.'

'Who?'

'You know. Minerva. She answered your message and told us where to get the Pentacorn Milk and the TangBang tree juice.'

'Oh, right! Yes, that's not a bad idea.' What did they

have to lose? He composed a Technomessage on the spot.

To: *Minerva*
From: *Shadow Demon*
Please can you tell me how to make money quickly. I have hardly got any TN left at all and my Flagondra is hungry. Please help. Thank you very much.

'There we are,' he said, pressing **Send**. 'Let's go and see Sabine and check back here in half an hour or so.'

Sabine was in her house, splashing around in the bath. Josh picked up the Slinky and set it off climbing down the stairs, and straightaway the dragon scrambled out to watch, shaking herself vigorously and sending drops flying everywhere. It *had* been irresponsible of Molly to spend all their money on toys, and Josh was going to have to watch her much more closely in future, but in a way he could understand. Sabine loved toys so much. She loved everything you gave her – well, almost everything, he thought, remembering the starsword. And these tiny, perfect replicas of full-sized toys were so fascinating. For the first time, Josh began to understand the attraction of a doll's house, of a world with everything in miniature.

'Minerva must have had enough time to answer by now,' Molly said.

'She might not be logged on,' said Josh. 'If she's in America she wouldn't even have finished school yet. Or work,' he added, because he had no real way of telling Minerva's age.

'In America they go to school in the evenings?'

'No, Molly, their clocks are on a different time. Didn't you know that?'

Molly shook her head. 'How d'you mean, a different time? I don't understand.'

'Well, when it's seven o'clock here, it's something like two o'clock there. Actually America is so big that it isn't even the same time all across it. It can be two o'clock in one part and four o'clock in another.'

'So what time do they show the six o'clock news?' asked Molly, and Josh couldn't think of any answer to that.

There was a reply waiting for them in their TechnoMailbox.

To: *Shadow Demon*
From: *Minerva*
Dear dear! This won't do at all. We can't have a helpless young Flagondra starving.
There are several ways to make Technickels. Best is to go into trade, but this takes a while before it becomes profitable. If you do become a merchant, try to become a specialist. I deal in spices, and I make more than 1000 TN most days by trading them. However, though you might be wise to think about this for the future, your current situation sounds too urgent.
You can, of course, try out the Lucky Star Casino, buy tickets for the Technolottery or go to the track and bet on Luponio races. You might make money at any of these, but it's far more likely that you'll lose the little you have.
You could try begging in the town centre.
Occasionally you'll get a real windfall – as much as

500 TN has been known – but normally people will just toss 1 or 2 TN at you. It is time-consuming and boring, and sometimes the police turn up and fine you.

You could enter your Flagondra in some competitions. But I think it's still very young and probably not much good at anything other than being cute. And unfortunately there are thousands and thousands of other baby Technomon just as cute as yours, though as a proud parent I'm sure you wouldn't agree with that!

Which leaves the games. Most of the games take a long time and pay poorly, as you may have discovered. But there are a couple of exceptions. If you happen to have a photographic memory you can make a fortune playing Memory Match. If not, have a go at CipherMaster, at which you should be able to make 100 TN in about 15 minutes, if you're reasonably competent.

Good luck!

'I *love* Minerva!' Molly said, when Josh had finished reading this aloud. 'Minerva *rules*!'

'She certainly does,' said Josh, clicking on **Reply** and composing a hasty message of thanks.

'So are you going to play those games now?'

'I'll give them a try, yes. But don't stand there watching over my shoulder, Molly.' Molly's face fell. 'I'm not being mean,' Josh said. 'It puts me off, that's all. You go and tire Sabine out with her new toys, and maybe she'll sleep tonight.' Sabine's nocturnal tendencies were an ongoing problem. Molly swore that she didn't mind, that she loved being up with the dragon during the night, but it left her falling asleep at all kinds of odd moments during the day, and sooner or later someone was going to start asking difficult questions. 'We'll meet up in half an hour. OK?'

'OK,' said Molly, skipping off upstairs.

Josh tried Memory Match first. It was one of those games where you have to turn up cards two at a time, and the aim is to turn up a pair that match. In this version all the cards had pictures of Technomon on them, and you were shown the layout face up for a few seconds at the beginning of each level. Josh saw what Minerva meant about having a photographic memory. If you could memorise the whole board just like that, you'd be able to pick off all the pairs perfectly, without making a single mistake, and progress to the next level with a whacking time bonus.

Josh, of course, could not do this. The first few levels, which had twelve, then sixteen, then twenty cards, gave him no trouble. If he was really quick he could clear them half by memory and half by trial and error. But round about Level Six (thirty-two cards) he started to become unstuck. In seven attempts at Memory Match he only cleared Level Six once, for which he was awarded a pathetic, an *insulting*, 10 Technickels. You couldn't even buy a packet of Trouble Gum for that!

Oh well. So he didn't have a photographic memory. He supposed if he had one he'd have known it by now, but all the same it was hard not to feel the faintest twinge of disappointment.

So it would have to be CipherMaster.

But as soon as he loaded up CipherMaster his spirits

sank, because it was a version of a game he'd come across before, and he'd never yet managed to get the hang of it. The computer generated a secret code consisting of four jewels, each of which could be any one of six types. Josh had to work out the code by submitting guesses, which the computer would mark for him, awarding him a gold star for each correct jewel in the correct place, and a silver star for a jewel that was the right type but in the wrong position. And the only way to progress to the next level was to solve the code within the time limit.

Josh gave it a go. He chose *ruby, emerald, sapphire, diamond*. The computer gave him one gold star and two silver. What should he do now? Any of the jewels could be right and any of them could be wrong! The timer ticked away. Josh began to panic. He tried *emerald, pearl, pearl, diamond*, not really knowing why, and this time he got two silver stars.

Josh stared at the screen, feeling miserably stupid. He had absolutely no idea what to do next. By now there was little more than a minute remaining. He chose *sapphire, sapphire, sapphire, sapphire*, feeling as he did so rather like a spoilt kid who isn't winning the game and so starts stamping their feet and breaking the rules. The computer shrugged and returned one gold star. By now Josh couldn't remember what a gold star even meant.

Time up! trilled the computer, revealing the answer: *ruby, sapphire, emerald, pearl*. Josh looked at his guesses and back to the solution, trying to figure how he could have got from one to the other, but when your brain's gone into spoiled brat mode it's hard to recover straightaway, and he simply couldn't work it out.

Molly came in to find him slumped in dejection in front of the screen, which was flashing the words: **Play Again? Play Again?** almost like a taunt.

'Never mind,' she said.

'But, Molly, this is a disaster. I needed to be able to play this game! It's the only game you can win at!'

'So can't you get someone to teach it to you?'

'Oh yeah, right. It's that easy. Someone like who?'

'I don't know! Don't you know anybody who plays games?'

'Of course I don't . . .' began Josh, but before he could finish the sentence, he realised that he did.

17

'Mastermind,' said William Beresford.

Josh wondered if he was being sarcastic. He said nothing.

'That's what that game's called,' William said. 'Mastermind.'

'Oh! Right, I get you. So – you know it, then?'

'We've had a set at home all my life,' said William. He didn't actually say 'and therefore I know everything there is to know about the game', but William Beresford being William Beresford, it seemed highly probable that he did.

Josh wasn't quite sure what to say next. Should he invite William, and his Mastermind set, round to their house? It would probably be the politest thing. But with a constantly crying baby, the whole family out for dinner almost every evening and a growing dragon in the bedroom, Josh's wasn't exactly the kind of household to which you automatically invited people back to visit.

And he could hardly invite himself to William's. That was way too pushy, especially when he'd barely spoken a single word to him until today.

Luckily William had ideas of his own.

'There's a set here, too,' he said.

'Here in school? Where?'

'In the Games Club cupboard. You'd better come along to Games Club. I can teach you there.'

'When's Games Club?' Josh felt slightly foolish. He'd been at this school his entire life and William less than a term. There shouldn't be things that William knew and he didn't. It wasn't right.

'Tuesday and Thursday lunchtimes,' said William. Josh pulled a face. It was Monday. 'And any other day if it's raining,' William added, with the faintest ghost of a smile. It was bucketing down outside.

'OK – well, great! Thanks! See you lunchtime, then.' There was a quality about William Beresford that made it hard for Josh to relax around him. He never had the slightest idea what he was thinking. 'Oh – by the way . . . '

'Yes?'

'*Where's* Games Club?'

'Mr Bailey's room,' said William, and disappeared down the corridor.

'Mr Beresford!' said Mr Bailey, looking up from his newspaper as Josh and William entered the room. 'Come to slaughter me at chess yet again? I've been studying the Sicilian over the weekend. You may be in for a very nasty surprise. And what's this?' He gave Josh a long look. 'Mr Harper, I do believe! Not a face I ever expected to see in here.'

'Josh wants to learn Mastermind,' said William. 'I'll slaughter you at chess tomorrow, if that's convenient.'

'It's extremely inconvenient,' said Mr Bailey. 'But I suppose I have no choice.' Josh was considerably taken aback by all of this. The version of Mr Bailey that inhabited the Games Room seemed altogether different from the one who patrolled the playground breaking up fights, and stalked the corridors keeping order.

William pointed to a table by the window. 'Sit down there. I'll find the game.' Josh sat, meekly, casting a furtive eye around the room. People were sitting in twos playing chess and draughts, and a crowd had gathered around what he thought was a backgammon board. In the far corner, a group from another class in Josh's year was engrossed in a game of Monopoly. How had Josh never known about Games Club? The truth was, of course, that he *had* known, in the way you can know about something in the outskirts of your vision, without ever paying it enough attention to bring it into focus.

William returned with the Mastermind set and sat down opposite. 'You know more or less how it works?' Josh nodded. This game had coloured pegs instead of jewels, and the markers were black and white pegs, not gold and silver stars, but none of that was anything more than decoration. The actual gameplay was identical.

'Now let me check I've got this right,' said William. 'You need to solve the code as fast as possible, rather than in as few guesses as possible.'

Josh nodded. 'There's a time limit. You do get bonus points for using fewer guesses, but that's not as important as solving it in the time. Because the bonuses get bigger the longer you play without losing.'

'OK. And you can take as many guesses as you like?'

'There's only room for ten.'

'That should be enough. OK. Don't look.' William dipped his hand into the box of coloured pegs, stirred them round a bit and picked out four. These he placed in holes in a secret alcove, where Josh couldn't see them. The four pegs formed the code he had to guess.

Josh tried *red yellow blue green*, earning one black peg and two white. He looked at these gloomily. White pegs were so tricky. They were supposed to be a help but in fact they caused nothing but confusion.

'I never know what to do next,' he said.

'If I were you I wouldn't have started like that,' William said, nodding toward *red yellow blue green*. 'Not if you're playing against the clock. Just bash out something simple. Keep it to just two colours.'

'Really? OK.' Josh set out *red blue red blue*.

'Much too fussy,' said William. 'You're not here to design a pretty pattern. Put them two and two. It's easier to keep track.'

Josh sheepishly re-arranged to *red red blue blue*, and William awarded him two black pegs. This was encouraging! Two colours in the right place!

'Now, bring in just one more colour,' said William. 'Always keep it simple. Guess which two pegs you got right – it's a *total* guess at this stage – and swap the other two with a new colour.'

Josh played *red orange blue orange*, and was given two black marker pegs and one white.

'What does that tell you?' William asked.

'Two pegs in the right place and one that's the right colour and in the wrong place.'

'Right. So what do you think now about the red and blue you kept from the first line?'

'I've still got two black so they're probably right,' said Josh.

'Wrong,' said William. 'Look again.'

Josh had to look for a couple of minutes before he got the point. 'Oh! I see. They can't both be right because then it would be impossible for you to have given me a white marker peg.'

'Good! The only other colour you've used is orange, so there's nowhere to move an orange to that isn't orange already.' He looked pleased, and somewhat surprised, that Josh had worked this out by himself. 'Now make another guess.'

Josh frowned, cupping his chin with his hands and concentrating as hard as he knew how. 'So I know there's one orange somewhere. There has to be. There might even be two but let's say there's one. So because I got three colours right in the last row the blue and the red must be right.'

'But . . . ?'

'But one of them has to move. And one of the oranges has to be swapped with a new colour.' Josh decided to move the blue and bring in yellow, and played *red orange yellow blue*.

'Inspired guesswork,' said William, giving him three black marker pegs. 'Beginner's luck.'

'Three right!'

'So which is going to be wrong?'

'I bet it's the new colour,' said Josh, replacing the

yellow with a green.

'Ta-da!' said William, revealing his hidden code, *red orange green blue*. 'That wasn't bad at all.' Josh would have taken bets that William was thinking: 'Hmmm! Not as dumb as I thought,' although a boy as polite as William would never dream of saying this.

'Right, let's start again,' said William, setting up a new code, and shaking his head sadly when Josh played *green green orange orange*.

'But you said to start off with two sets of two . . .'

'Use the same colour scheme every time. You're playing against the clock here. If you always start with red and blue, and bring in orange third, then yellow fourth, you'll never have to stop and think about it. It'll save you seconds. I promise.'

'But if you know how I'm going to start you'll know how to trick me!'

'But you're not going to be playing against me! You're playing against a computer! It isn't going to make notes of your guesses. It'll just mark them and forget them. And anyway, you can't trick someone at this game. It's pure logic.'

William, it seemed, thought of everything. Josh didn't argue. He just played *red red blue blue*, and off they went again.

By the end of their half hour Josh was stunned at how much he'd learned. The same positions and rules kept on coming up, and he'd done a pretty good job of learning them. He could hardly wait to get his hands on CipherMaster. He would earn bucketsful of Technickels and let Molly buy anything she liked for Sabine! He glowed in advance, just thinking about it. For a glorious moment all his troubles were forgotten.

Mr Bailey came over just before the bell rang. 'Well,' he said. 'Did you enjoy your visit?'

Josh said he had, very much.

'We don't get much demand for Mastermind usually,' said Mr Bailey.

'He needed to learn it for some competition on the Internet,' William said, and Mr Bailey said: 'Ah, the *Inter*net! And shall we be seeing you back here tomorrow?'

Josh hoped that William would say, 'Of course you must come tomorrow!' but William's face was unreadable as he waited for Josh's reply. So Josh said: 'Well, I was thinking if I make mistakes playing CipherMaster tonight, I could make a note of it, and perhaps you could tell me what I should have done?' and William said that would be fine; that he had promised Mr Bailey a game of chess, but that it didn't usually take long to beat Mr Bailey, so he expected he could fit Josh in as well. And far from being offended or cross, Mr Bailey gave William an amused little punch and told him to be careful, that perhaps he (Mr Bailey) had been softening him up for the kill, waiting for William to suggest they start playing for money, at which point Mr Bailey, who was secretly a Grand Master, would start to play properly, wiping out William and his entire family and causing them to be destitute and homeless. William raised his eyebrows and said, 'Yeah, *right*!', and Josh, more and more amazed by this conversation, decided on the spot that he would be returning to Games Club, this parallel universe right on the doorstep where people he saw every day behaved in entirely different ways, as often as he possibly could.

18

That evening Josh played CipherMaster for forty-five minutes after they all got back from dinner at Pizza Hut, where Luke had smiled and gurgled and drunk his milk and acted for all the world like a regular baby, though of course when they'd arrived back home he'd soon started to cry. The whole business of Luke's crying patterns was starting to cause a dark, unwanted thought to form itself in a distant corner of Josh's mind, but for the most part it was so far back that he could avoid looking directly at it.

It was so much more pleasant to think about CipherMaster, at which he had just managed to win 228 Technickels! Almost half as much as they'd ever had! So much weight dropped off his shoulders, Josh felt almost as though he had risen to float a few inches above the floor. He could do this every single night. Often he'd be able to play for longer, and his skills would improve further, and all of a sudden earning 500 Technickels a day seemed a perfectly realistic target.

Which made Technopolis their very own toy factory. They'd be able to order scaled-down versions of almost anything you could find in the real world. Furniture, electronics, jewellery, flowers – you name it, somewhere in Technopolis, there would be a shop that sold it. The possibilities were endless, and not just for Sabine, although perhaps in a week or two they really could think of getting her that motor go-kart. Josh would be able to buy his mother a bunch of perfect miniature roses. Imagine her astonishment as she wondered how anyone could possibly have grown flowers so small. And then she would think of course they must be artificial, and laugh at herself for her own mistake, until a few days later when the petals started to wither and fade…

He let Molly buy anything she wanted: a basketball hoop, a pogo stick, a trampoline. She went to the clothes store and ordered a baseball cap for Sabine. For an extra 10 TN per letter, you could order a name of up to five letters stitched on your cap. 'Sabine' was too long, so they decided to have a plain 'S' – white on a blue background. Josh knew before he even saw it that the stitching would be perfect. It always was. They were asked to type in Sabine's breed and weight, and when the cap arrived, not only did it fit, but it had holes in exactly the right places to accommodate a pair of Flagondra ears.

They bought Sabine a luxury dinner – rocky sizzlers, a triple decker barbecue special from *Beachburgers*, a giant-size starfruit fizz and, of course, a frosted double choc chip fudge gourmet snowball.

'Fat!' Josh said affectionately, rubbing Sabine's tummy after her meal. The dragon let out a tremendous burp. 'Greedy!'

'We did buy her all her favourite things,' said Molly. 'You can't blame her.'

'Workout time!' Josh said sternly. 'You have to keep

fit! Where's your football?' Sabine gave a little quiver of excitement at the word 'football'.

'All the new stuff must have arrived!' said Molly. 'I'd forgotten!' They had become so used to deliveries from Technopolis that nowadays they rarely even bothered trying to watch them arrive. Molly went over to check the mousemat, gave a squeal of triumph, and returned with Sabine's new sports gear gathered in her arms.

'Better not let her on the trampoline just now,' Josh said, looking up. 'I think if she bounced she might burst.'

'Maybe basketball then?' asked Molly, and Josh nodded. Sabine's ball skills were superb. Already she could juggle with three balls for seven or eight catches in a row, and she was improving every day. She'd be brilliant at basketball. Josh knew it.

Sabine had only just caught sight of her new things. Her wings fluttered and she gave one of her squeaks of rapture, except that this one sounded more like a croak.

Molly looked up. 'Has she got a cough? We could get her some Cough Remedy from *Morgana's Apothecary*. It's made from lumbus weed and chuckleberry syrup.'

'I don't think she's got a cough. I think her voice is just getting deeper.' Josh had thought this was something that only happened to boys, but maybe dragons were different. Sabine made the croaking noise again, and this time she opened her mouth as she did it and a spark flew out.

'Josh! She's on fire!'

But Josh knew what was happening. 'Molly. She's a *dragon*. Dragons . . . breathe flames. She must be getting old enough to start.'

'Ohhhh!' Molly gazed at Sabine with awe. 'Sabine! Do it again! Make fire!' But Sabine could only manage a dry, hoarse, throaty noise, which sounded as if it was hurting her.

'Don't encourage her, Molly!' said Josh.

'But I want to see her do it!'

'You want her breathing fire? Just think about it. She's alone in the house for hours every day. One *whooooosh!* of flames and the doll's house would catch alight, and soon the whole room would be on fire and when we got back our home would be burned to the ground. Is that what you want to happen?'

'I'll tell her she's not allowed,' said Molly.

'Well, what if she forgets? What if she can't even help herself? Perhaps it's like sneezing. Perhaps the flames build up inside her and irritate her nose and throat until she *has* to let them out.'

Molly said nothing.

'Molly. We're going to have to start thinking about the future. It's not just that she's going to be a fire hazard. Look at her wings. She's trying to flap them already.' Josh tapped one of the dragon's wings, which immediately fluttered upwards. The paper-thin membrane looked so fragile that Josh was terrified he might stab through it by accident with a fingernail.

'So?' said Molly.

'So she's going to want to fly! It's not fair to keep a flying creature cooped up in a doll's house. And anyway she's getting too big for the doll's house.'

'She can fly around the room,' Molly said mutinously.

'And anyway, she can go out of the window and have her adventures and then come back. I know I can train her to come back. She always does as she's told.'

'Molly, if she flies out of the window she'll probably get eaten. Some big bird will drop from the sky and carry her off in its claws. Or she'll land in a garden and explore and a cat will pounce on her and torture her for hours before it finally kills her, because that's what cats do! Is *that* what you want to happen?'

Molly burst into tears. Sabine looked from one of them to the other in bewilderment. She'd been expecting a game, and she'd been so pleased and excited, and now everything had gone wrong and it was Josh's fault as usual. 'Molly,' he said. 'I'm sorry. I wasn't trying to be mean. I just wanted you to *think*!'

Molly tried to say something but she was still crying too much for Josh to make it out. Sabine began to wail. Any possibility of fun had disappeared. Only half an hour earlier they'd been bubbling over with joy, and somehow Josh had ruined everything.

But sometimes you *had* to think about unpleasant things. Molly never would, so Josh had to do all the worrying for both of them, and somehow this always ended up making him the bad guy. It was so unfair. He didn't *enjoy* worrying, but somebody had to take some responsibility or anything could happen!

You would think that having a baby dragon to care for would be the most wonderful thing in the world. But now that the initial excitement had worn off, Sabine was causing so much hard work and anxiety. It was like having a new baby, except at least with a baby you didn't have to figure out how to cope when it started to take to the air and set fire to things. They'd only just solved the Technickels problem, and already another two had sprung up to replace it. The difficulties were bound to grow in magnitude as Sabine grew herself, and Josh was exhausted from trying to find so many answers.

The full flood of Molly's crying had exhausted itself, and she and Sabine were now sniffling together in what Josh suddenly thought of as a very girly way, flashing him little hurt glances. He knew when it was time to leave.

Downstairs, the house was silent.

Josh peeked into the kitchen. Empty.

He found his mother asleep in front of the television. There was no sign of his father or Luke anywhere. They must have gone out for another soothing drive. A quick look out the front showed that his father's car was gone. Josh stood outside for a few minutes, feeling suddenly very alone under the silent night sky. Then he went indoors, logged into Technopolis and earned another 514 Technickels playing CipherMaster. The game made him think so hard that all his worries were, for the moment, forgotten, and Josh played on and on until he was too tired to remember how.

'I don't believe it!' Mr Bailey said, looking down at the chessboard with horror. 'My position has collapsed.'

'You shouldn't have exchanged bishops,' said William Beresford. 'You're always much too keen to exchange pieces.'

'I like a nice uncluttered board,' Mr Bailey said defensively.

'Yes, but I know that now,' William said. 'And so I can lure you into doing things that aren't in your best interest. And then look what happens.' He pointed at the board, Mr Bailey's white king under siege in a corner, William's own king securely guarded by a small black army of pieces at the other end.

'I resign,' Mr Bailey said with a deep sigh. 'Again. Well, Mr Harper, what did you think of that?'

'Very interesting,' said Josh.

'Would you like a game?'

'Oh no – I can't really play very well,' Josh said hurriedly. 'I'm still learning.' The truth was that he barely knew how the pieces moved, but hadn't wanted to admit that in case they sent him away. And it had been interesting, even if he didn't understand the chess. The fascinating thing for Josh was watching William and Mr Bailey. He had never realised it was possible for a teacher and a pupil to treat each other as equals. He had the feeling that they would have been perfectly delighted to meet up and play each other at chess *out* of school, for all the world as if they were friends.

'Josh wants to look at a few more Mastermind positions,' William explained. Josh had been woken early by Luke's cries as someone carried him past his bedroom, and for once had been unable to drift straight back into sleep, so he'd got up and played another hour and a quarter of CipherMaster. He was starting to wonder if he was getting addicted. It was so wonderfully calming. Not only did the game blot out all his problems by requiring every ounce of his concentration, but all the hundreds of Technickels mounting up in the bank gave Josh a wonderful feeling of security. He had already made so much money that he could take two weeks off without Sabine's luxurious lifestyle being threatened in the slightest. Josh couldn't immediately see any reason why he would want to take two weeks off, but it was a cruel uncertain world and you never knew. The computer might break down. *Damn!* That was something else to worry about, because without the computer they couldn't get hold of any dragon food. How had he managed to overlook *that*? Clearly he hadn't been worrying enough, or else he would have thought of it. The idea that he might need to worry *more* made Josh feel almost faint. He made a mental note to lay down a stock of non-perishable foodstuffs for Sabine, the moment he got home, and then immediately started to worry that the tiny can-opener available from the Technopolis hardware store would be too small for him or Molly to use.

'In that case I'll wander over and take a look at the backgammon,' said Mr Bailey, and Josh pulled out the piece of paper on which he'd noted down the positions of the pegs on the games where he'd failed to solve the code within the time. He'd done it very neatly with coloured pens; William gave a nod of approval and Josh glowed with pride.

They worked through all the positions in ten minutes. 'Thanks,' Josh said, though it didn't really seem like enough. Where should he go from here, with William Beresford? Was this to be the end of their connection, and if so did that mean the end of Games Club for Josh? The end of watching chess, and of whatever else might go on in this safe little world, a haven from the torments that so often lurked outside?

And at that very moment, as if to emphasise the point, the face of Shane Walters appeared at the window, contorted into a hideous grimace, and rapidly registering surprise at the sight of Josh sitting there with William. Two seconds later Dylan Brasher appeared as well; they exchanged some comments the nature of which Josh could all too well imagine, and burst into mocking laughter. Mr Bailey looked over and stood up, and the faces disappeared at once, but Josh felt sure they hadn't heard the end of this. Two of Shane and Dylan's favourite victims, caught together! No good could possibly come of it.

'Cretins,' said William, with a surprising note of savagery.

Josh sighed. 'You've only had them for a term. I've had them my entire life. At least now it's only till July. Just the rest of this week and then one more term. Next year all that lot are going to Gresham Park and I'll never see them again.'

'Where are you going next year, then?' asked William, and 'Kingsbury,' Josh answered.

'*Really?*'

'Yes, really. Why?'

'That's where I'm going,' William said.

'*Really?*'

'We're going round in circles here. Yes, really. Why are you so surprised?'

'Well.' Josh didn't know quite how to put it into words. 'I just thought – well, you've always seemed like some kind of genius. I thought there was some special school for people like you.' He was half-afraid that William would take offence at this, but he just laughed.

'Genius Academy? There's no such thing. There's only selective schools, and that's what Kingsbury is. The entrance exam is quite tough. That's why I didn't realise – I mean – um...'

It was William's turn to be concerned that he'd given offence.

'You didn't think I was smart enough to get in?'

'Oh, God. I'm sorry,' William said. 'It sounds so insulting. But – you know – since I've been here you haven't given me any particular reason to think you were that smart. I don't want to be rude, but there's no other way to put it. It was only yesterday when I was explaining Mastermind to you that I began to realise you actually had something of a brain in there.'

'It's OK,' Josh said. 'I haven't been at all smart for a few months now.' It was true. He'd been pretty messed up ever since Christmas. So much had gone wrong. Luke had arrived so early, turning their family upside down and causing their mother virtually to move out and live in the hospital. Claudio had left for Italy, leaving Josh without his best friend and protector. And then, most recently, there had been Sabine...

He couldn't tell William about the dragon and he still didn't like talking about Luke outside the family, but it seemed safe to explain about Claudio.

'Ah,' said William. 'So *that's* why you looked so horrified at the thought of me being put to sit next to you. The seat was still warm from your best friend.'

Josh twisted up inside and his cheeks burned with shame. 'I'm sorry,' he said lamely. 'I didn't realise you'd noticed. Honestly. And it wasn't anything to do with *you*. It was just that . . . '

'Don't look so agonised,' said William. 'You don't need to explain. I understand. I'd have felt exactly the same way myself.'

'Really?'

'Here we go again with the reallys. Yes, really! And now, am I going to teach you chess or not?'

'Oh! Well – yes, please!'

'Good. Because I was beginning to wonder if you were ever going to ask.' William collected up all the pieces and began to set them out on the board. 'This is a lot harder than Mastermind. There's a lot to take in. But as a beginner, there's one golden rule you must always remember above all others, which is this: never, never *ever*, listen to anything Mr Bailey tells you.'

'I heard that!' roared Mr Bailey from across the room, and Josh moved to his old seat opposite William, suddenly flooded with happiness as he settled down to his first lesson at chess.

19

One of Molly's nicer points was that forgiving and forgetting came as second nature to her. The row last night would have blown over by the morning, but unfortunately they'd had another row straightaway when Josh insisted on spraying the whole of the inside of the doll's house with water as a precaution in case Sabine started breathing flame while they were at school. Molly had stumbled over all tousled and sleepy and grouchy, and started hitting him, yelling that he had no right to go ruining her furnishings like that, and Josh had yelled back that wet things would dry but burned things stayed burned forever, and Molly had started crying again. It wasn't like Molly to be so fragile, and when she told Josh on the way home that she had a note for their mother, it didn't take a genius to work out what the note was likely to say.

'Molly. Have you been falling asleep in class again?'

Molly bit her lip and nodded. 'They've been trying to phone home but nobody ever answers. So I got this note instead.'

'Well, that's not surprising. Nobody's ever in. Molly – look – you can't go on like this. No, don't look at me like that. You just can't. We'll have to take it turns having Sabine in our room at night. Like Mum and Dad take it in turns with Luke. It's too much for you on your own.'

'But I'm hardly ever awake!' Molly said stubbornly. 'Maybe a few times in the night she wakes me up but I fall right back to sleep again.'

'I bet you don't.'

'I do! The rest of the time she plays by herself. Last night she was practising basketball for hours. She's got really good already.'

'Molly! You mean you let her out at night? She's out loose in the room?'

'Well, of course she is! You can't expect her to stay shut in her house all day while we're at school *and* all night! That would be a terrible life!'

Objections were flooding into Josh's mind. 'But what if Mum or Dad heard her? They'd just walk in and see her!'

'Luke's always crying in the night,' Molly said. 'They never hear a thing.'

'And anyway, how would you know she played basketball for hours if you weren't awake to see?' No wonder Sabine had grown so skilful at football and juggling and everything. She was getting hours and hours of practice that Josh had never known about. 'Molly, I'm serious. This has to stop! Tonight we move the house into my room. No! Don't argue! We'll move her back in the morning before school. Nobody will ever know the difference. I don't think anybody but us has been in our bedrooms all week anyway,' he added. The Harper household had more or less given up cleaning. Nobody had the energy.

When they got home Mum and Luke were sitting out

in the garden, down the far end by the shed, fast asleep. This happened quite a lot if it wasn't raining. It wasn't really surprising, Josh thought, wandering out to take a look at them. Luke was awake all night and Mum was awake half the night with him. They had to catch up wherever they could.

His mother was stretched out on a sunbed, folded up to a more or less sitting position, and she'd covered herself with a duvet, for it was still only March. Mum could catch up on some sleep during the day, but how on earth was his father managing at work? Josh's father never complained but he was acting more and more like a zombie, like a sleepwalker. Two parents simply weren't enough for a baby that didn't sleep at night, thought Josh. You needed three or four. This thought brought up the unpleasant spectre of Grandma Helen moving in, so he'd never spoken it aloud. He'd offered to take a shift himself but this had been refused. 'You need your sleep! You're a growing boy and you need to be up early for school.' Josh was sure he could grow equally well while he was awake, but all the same he was quite relieved to be turned down, because minding Luke on his own made him nervous.

And again the words, 'We can't go on like this', so recently spoken to his sister, formed themselves inside his head.

He leaned over his brother and softly touched his cheek. Luke stirred slightly and made a faint sound, and Josh suddenly thought: he doesn't look like a sick baby, a premature baby, an ill baby any more, he just looks like a regular baby! It was such an astonishing thought that he took another long look, just to make sure. Luke's eyelashes fluttered slightly. His cheeks had filled out, and were a healthy pink. You could almost call them *rosy*.

'You're not ill at all, are you?' Josh said. He'd suspected it for some days, and now he was sure. 'You don't cry all night because you're ill. You never did have colic. You cry because you're irritated. Because you're *annoyed*.' Luke slept on.

Josh understood everything now. He'd suspected for a while and now he knew it was true. He was filled with a heavy sadness, though 'filled' was the wrong word altogether, because the sadness was draining him empty.

He went back into the house. Molly's schoolbag was lying in the hall where she'd tossed it in her scramble upstairs to Sabine. Josh opened it, found the letter from school, and slid it inside a huge untidy pile of post and papers that had been building up against the wall. He put it two-thirds of the way down. It was very unlikely to be found for some days, and by then it would be too late to matter.

The doorbell rang.

Josh opened it, and there stood a young woman he'd never seen before, with Luke in his carryseat. Luke? *What?* And then he looked more closely and saw that it was another, identical carryseat, containing a different baby altogether.

'Hello. You must be Josh,' said the woman.

'Yes. Erm – did you want to see Mum?'

'If I could. She left Luke's cardigan at our house

yesterday and I had to drive over this way so I thought I'd stop and drop it off.'

'Thank you very much,' Josh said politely, though it sounded to him like an excuse. Luke had dozens of cardigans, and if all this woman wanted to do was to hand this one back, she'd have left the baby in the car. But she'd gone to all the trouble of unstrapping it, and that meant she expected to be invited in. He noticed, in her other hand, a brightly coloured bag of the kind used to carry round nappies and wipes and bottles and toys for travelling and visits. This was definitely intended as a visit.

'My name's Caitlin, by the way,' the woman said, peeking over Josh's head inside the house. 'Is that Molly?' Josh turned. His sister was on the landing, peeking through the staircase with curiosity.

'Hello,' Molly said, coming down to join them. 'Oh, is that your baby? What's her name?'

'Rhiannon,' said the woman Caitlin. Rhiannon, who had been surveying Josh with a pair of beady blue eyes, transferred her gaze to Molly.

'Isn't she lovely!' said Molly.

Josh couldn't put it off any longer. 'Would you like to come in? Mum's in the garden. I could go and get her.'

'I don't want to be any trouble,' said Caitlin, but even as she spoke she was lifting the carryseat inside the house and looking inquisitively all around. The hall was a tip. Clothes were scattered all the way up the staircase. The pile of papers had spilt over at the top, other pieces of household junk were scattered across the floor, and just outside the kitchen door was a spilt bowl of cereal, milk soaked into the carpet, the cereal congealed into lumps on the surface.

There simply wasn't any time for cleaning up during the week. Every spare second had to be devoted to sleeping. But Josh certainly wasn't going to start explaining this to Caitlin, especially as the baby Rhiannon had just let out an ear-splitting wail of distress, as if the sluttishness of the Harpers' domestic arrangements were proving intolerable to her tender sensibilities.

'Come out the back,' he said, opening the door and ushering them through. Mum's eyes had already opened at the sound of a baby's cry; she had turned to Luke straightaway, and was now looking puzzled to find him still deep in sleep.

'Mum!' Josh called. 'You've got a visitor.'

'Oh! Caitlin! Oh, my goodness – what a surprise!' Nobody had visited for such a long time. Caitlin explained again about the cardigan, and Mum said it was so kind of her but really she needn't have bothered (absolutely! thought Josh), and she really must stop for a coffee.

They all went back inside the kitchen, where Josh's mother gave a sudden gasp of horror at the sight of the mess it was in. Nobody had washed up since the weekend. Discarded bottles and bibs littered the floor. On the table, a carton of orange juice had been knocked over and the spillage, pooling on the table, had flowed all down to the ground, creating a sticky, orange, hazardous patch of gunge.

‘Don’t worry!’ Caitlin said brightly, picking up the vibes. ‘I know what it’s like, with a baby! You ought to see my kitchen!’ Yeah, right, thought Josh, who was certain that Caitlin’s house was squeaky clean and shiny as a brand new pin.

Both babies began yelling at the same moment.

Caitlin frowned. ‘But Rhiannon never cries!’

Josh was starting to take a dislike to Caitlin and her perfect house and her perfect baby. ‘They’d be happier out in the garden,’ he said. ‘That’s what babies like. Nice fresh air.’

Caitlin gave him a look that said, ‘Oh, so now you think you know more about my baby than I do?’

Josh picked up his own baby’s carryseat, said: ‘Watch!’ and took Luke out to the garden, plonking the seat down halfway along the path. Luke fell silent straightaway.

‘It does honestly seem to work,’ Mum said. ‘Let’s just try it with Rhiannon.’

Caitlin looked dubious, but was persuaded to take her baby outside and park her opposite Luke.

Rhiannon’s sobs died away almost instantly, and she set about the important business of examining Luke. Josh had noticed before how babies will latch on to the sight of a human face and stare unblinkingly at it for ages. However, he’d never before seen two babies engaged in a staring contest. ‘Come on now, Luke,’ he said, as Mum and Caitlin retreated indoors, with much muttering and anxious backward looks. ‘You can win this! Don’t you let this perfect girl baby outstare you. Go! Go! Stick with it!’

Thirty interminable seconds passed, and then Rhiannon looked away.

'Yee-hah!!!!' Josh leaped up, high fiving in thin air. 'Wicked! You did it! You go, bro! You show this sissyass girl! You is da baddest baby!' And perhaps it was his imagination, but he could almost have sworn that he saw his brother's tiny lips stretch into a gleaming smile of triumph.

Josh left the Mother and Baby Club to do whatever they do, and joined Molly and Sabine for a skateboarding session. Sabine was starting to master some tricks; as Josh came into the room she pulled off her first perfect ollie. The tiny squashed bedraggled thing that had crawled out of the egg was by now scarcely recognisable. Sabine's size had more than doubled. She was a Level 9 Flagondra, with the extraordinarily high Agility rating of 38. Josh had been looking at other Flagondra on the website and he'd never seen another Level 9 with Agility higher than 23. They had given Sabine a good upbringing – nobody could say otherwise. She was bright and supremely talented and sunny-natured. She was happy.

And all of this was going to make what he had to say even harder. He tried to find the words but it was impossible to know even where to begin, and he was still trying things out in his mind when their mother called them downstairs to tell them how shocked and horrified she had been to have a friend see their house in this terrible state, and that she'd never felt so ashamed in her whole life, and that Grandma Helen was coming over tomorrow to spend the whole day cleaning and sorting out every single inch of their home from top to bottom.

Josh and Molly slunk back upstairs struck dumb by this news.

'What are we going to *do*?' Molly asked eventually. 'Grandma Helen will find Sabine. She finds everything. We have to hide her somewhere else.'

'There's nowhere we can hide her,' Josh said. 'Nowhere that would be safe.'

'Then what are we going to do?' Molly picked Sabine up and started crooning to her softly. Sabine lifted up her face for one of their nose-breathing kisses of affection, but this time Molly jumped, startled.

'Hot!'

'Molly, be careful! You can't put your face up close to hers like that any more. She's making sparks more and more often. Don't get upset about it,' he added, seeing his sister's face. 'It's just what dragons do. It's natural.' This would have been a good point to introduce the much-needed topic of Sabine's future, but Molly sniffed and said: 'So what about tomorrow, then?' and Josh answered: 'I'm just going to have to take her to school.'

20

It wasn't so very difficult. They still had the ice cream tub, air holes already punched into the lid. They lined it with bedding, and packed a bag of spuddly cheesies, two ripe firefruit, a carton of aubergine nectar and Teddy Sheringham, the turquoise bear. Sabine wouldn't be hungry, she wouldn't be thirsty, but goodness, wouldn't she be bored. Trapped all day in a tub nowhere near big enough. She could still just about stand up without her head grazing the lid, but she couldn't run about or exercise, and there was no way to light up the tub. She would be cramped in the dark all day, living in conditions no better than battery hens! And she was nocturnal so the dark wouldn't even make her sleepy.

There was only one answer. Molly and Josh didn't like it much, but they couldn't see that they had a choice. They went to *Morgana's Apothecary* in the Technopolis Shopping Arcade and bought a bottle of sleeping mixture.

'Contains spiratica noctis,' read Josh. 'Delicious minty taste. Dosage: one spoonful per 20g bodyweight.' The bottle had arrived with a measuring spoon.

'What does she weigh now?' Molly asked, drawing spirally doodles on a pad.

Josh clicked on **Your Pet**.

Type: Flagondra
Name: Sabine
Weight: 63 g
Height: 83 mm
Level: 9
Owner: Shadow Demon
Owner No: 6,666,666

'Three spoonfuls will be almost exactly right,' he said.

'It's going to be a horrible day for her,' Molly said mournfully, slumping forward on the desk and leaning her head on her arms.

'She'll sleep right through,' Josh said. He tried to sound as convincing as he could, as much for his own benefit as for Molly's. 'She won't know a thing about it. All she'll remember is sweet dreams of playing centre forward for Flagondra United and scoring a hat trick in the Technopolis Cup Final.'

That night he moved Sabine, her house and most of her toys into his own bedroom, and told Molly to be sure to get a good night's sleep.

'Well!' he said to Sabine. The dragon was sniffing around in a frenzy of excitement. This was where she'd been born, where she'd spent the first night of her life, and she hadn't been back since and all the old scents were driving her wild. She kept going back to the spot where she'd crawled out of the egg, which obviously smelled much the same as it had then. This just went to show how much cleaning had gone on in the meantime.

'I'm going to bed now,' Josh said, although he didn't expect to get much sleep. It was so hard to relax with the dragon roaming free around the room. He knew Sabine would always come when Molly called her, but then Molly could speak her language. Would she come for Josh? 'Sabine,' he said in a low, nervous voice. The dragon looked up but carried on bouncing her basketball. 'Sabine!' he said, more loudly this time, and patting the duvet by his side. This did the trick. Sabine scampered over to the bed, hauled herself up in an ungraceful scramble that pulled the duvet half down to the floor, and presented herself for praise.

'*Good* girl,' Josh said, scratching her under her chin and feeling much better. 'OK. Now you can go and play for a while.' Sabine looked blank. 'Play! With your toys. Down off the bed.' The dragon shuffled to the edge of the duvet, peeked over the edge and looked back at Josh hopefully.

'You can't get down? You can get up but not down?' Maybe that wasn't so surprising. Down was always scarier. 'Here comes your transport to the ground floor,' he said, putting a hand out for the dragon to climb on and then lowering it smoothly to the carpet. 'Ping! You have arrived at your destination.' Sabine ran off.

But then, five minutes later, she was back, and this time she brought the basketball. Oh well, Josh thought, sleepily. If you can play beach volleyball, then why not bed basketball? Sabine could leap and dive without any fear of landing awkwardly on a hard surface. Maybe all games should be played like this. Probably heaven was full of cloud basketball courts. Josh was just trying to remember if heaven had the same gravity as the moon, which would make the game *really* interesting, when he was woken up by Sabine pulling on his nose.

'Urmpph. Sabine. Go sleep.' But the dragon was wide awake and had no intention of letting him alone. Her ball had fallen off the edge of the bed.

'This is the last time I'm doing this!' Josh said, trying to sound stern, as he lifted her down. He didn't say Ping! this time in case it started to turn into one of those games she wanted to play over and over. 'Now off you go and play by yourself for a while. I need some rest.'

He was expecting resistance, but Sabine was ready for a break, and disappeared inside her house for a snack and a drink. As he drifted back to sleep, Josh thought he heard the sound of splashing in the bathwater, but he must have been wrong about that because here he was with the rest of his class at the swimming baths, and – now here was a strange and wonderful thing – the water was sloping down steeply from the deep end, which was a huge improvement on the usual system because you could actually see which end the deep end was. And water skiing would be so much more fun with a slope to ski down! Josh climbed out of the pool, followed by several Technomon clutching their surfboards, and paddled through the showers. 'This is all a terrible mistake,' said William Beresford from inside his giant alligator costume, and Josh was just about to explain about the wave machine when somebody poked him in the chin, and he woke up yet again to find Sabine back on the bed, asking to be put down to get her ball.

'No,' said Josh. 'Enough.'

Sabine gave one of her croaky squeaks and Josh saw sparks cracking like lightning at the back of her throat.

'No!' he said.

In all her short life nobody had ever said NO to Sabine and been able to stick to it. She was simply too cute to be resisted. And as a result, she didn't really grasp the concept of NO. She made her way to the edge of the bed and waited for Josh to give her a ride down on her own personal elevator, that sometimes went Ping! and sometimes was silent, but always, always worked.

Except that this time it didn't.

Sabine shuffled closer to the edge.

'Forget it,' said Josh, and tried to go back to sleep, but of course it was impossible, with Sabine tottering on the brink of a drop that was, for her, the equivalent of Josh falling off the top of a house. She could break every bone in her body. And what then? They could hardly take her to a vet! Josh sat upright, beginning to panic, and at that very moment Sabine, maybe assuming the movement to mean the arrival of a supporting hand, stepped forward into nothingness.

'No!' Josh dived across the bed to try and catch her, but he was too late. He closed his eyes in horror, waiting for a thump, a scream of pain, but he heard something altogether different: a furious flapping, which he knew, even before he opened his eyes, to be the beating of wings on air. Sabine was coasting the final few inches to the carpet. She had travelled halfway to the bedroom door in mid-air. As Josh watched, she touched down with a gentle bump, made a startled little *oof!* of surprise, and turned around to face him, beaming from ear to ear.

Well, who wouldn't? How does it feel to learn that you can fly?

Josh climbed out of bed and Sabine came running over all brimful of excitement, her wings still twitching.

'Woo-hoo!' he said, picking her up. He couldn't find any words that made sense. It was too thrilling. No wonder parents made such a fuss about seeing their kid walk for the first time! Poor Molly – she had missed it. The moment was gone forever. Perhaps he wouldn't tell her. All he had to do was to say nothing, and soon – tomorrow – today! it was already two thirty in the morning – Molly would see for herself, and she'd believe it was the first time, and why shouldn't she?

It could just be their little secret.

'Again?' he said to Sabine, and lifted her back onto the bed, perching her at the edge of the duvet, poised for take-off. He crawled backwards, held his hands out encouragingly, and the dragon paused only for a second before launching herself into the air and sailing across the room, straight into them.

All thoughts of sleep had disappeared.

Sabine slept soundly through the next morning, tucked up in the ice cream tub inside Josh's schoolbag. It had hardly seemed necessary to give her the sleeping medicine.

What was needed was staying-awake medicine for Josh. It got harder and harder to keep his eyes open as the hours passed. It was fortunate that his seat was right at the back of the room. He could bury his head in his hands as if he was concentrating intently on his work, and doze off without being spotted for two or three minutes, before waking with a jolt. There, he thought each time, now I'll be all right – but soon afterwards he would find himself drifting off once more. He tried to think of tricks to keep himself awake, like kicking himself once every twenty seconds, but of course he was too tired to remember to do it. He tried digging a fingernail into his palm as hard as he could, and the only difference it made was that the next time he woke he had a painful new-moon shaped gouge mark on his hand.

And then, just five minutes before the bell was due to ring for lunch, something happened that had Josh wide awake in seconds. A muffled noise, coming from his bag. Sabine had woken up.

Josh coughed. There was a brief silence, and then the noise came again. It was so soft that Josh wasn't even sure if anybody else could hear it, but he wasn't taking any chances. He coughed again, and again.

You can get away with one cough without attracting attention but three is too many. People began to look round over their shoulders. Shane Walters leaned forward and whispered something to Dylan Brasher, who smirked and flashed Josh a dirty look.

'You all right back there, Josh?' Miss Hollis asked, and: 'I think I've a got a cough,' Josh said, the sentence disappearing into a sort of chokey grunt as his schoolbag rustled again, more loudly this time. The whole classroom started to laugh, and it was a huge relief when, one minute later, the bell sounded at long last.

Josh grabbed the bag and raced off to the toilets, where he locked himself in and pulled out the ice cream tub. Sabine was not looking happy, and Josh couldn't say he blamed her. She cheered up slightly after a snack and a drink, but she wanted to be put down, and this couldn't be allowed. There was a gap at floor level between Josh's cubicle and the one next door, and some nasty looking damp patches on the ground. The dragon was wide awake now, and restless, and they still had the whole of the afternoon to get through. There was nothing for it but to give her another dose of sleeping mixture.

'I'm sorry,' he whispered, tipping the medicine into her mouth. 'I hate doing this. But it's only for today. You just have to sleep a few more hours and then all of this will be over.' The first dose had lasted about four hours, so this one should be enough to get them through.

Josh stayed with Sabine until she started yawning and curled back up again to sleep. He'd already missed lunch. He didn't much care about that. All he wanted was to lie down and rest. He couldn't honestly see how he was going to make it through the afternoon. He hadn't liked the way Dylan and Shane had been looking at him. He had a bad feeling that he really ought to keep his wits about him, and he wasn't even managing to keep his eyes open.

And then he had the most wonderful idea.

21

'Now you just lie quiet there and have a little rest and I'll come back in a while and see if you're feeling any better.'

Had any words ever been so welcome? Josh pulled the rough blanket up over his shoulders, turned to check on his bag which lay by his side just beneath the pillow, and surrendered. Sick Bay. Why hadn't he thought of it sooner? It had taken no effort at all to persuade Mrs Jackson that he was ill and needed to lie down. He looked ill. He looked like the walking dead. Two minutes later he was fast asleep, and the next thing he knew Mrs Jackson was back, saying she'd been in to see him several times but he was out like a light, and he'd slept so long that the final bell had rung and school was over, and did he want her to give his mum a ring or was he all right now?

'I'm OK,' Josh said, sitting up and rubbing his eyes.

'Perhaps you've got 'flu coming on,' Mrs Jackson said. 'It does knock the stuffing out of people. Miss Hollis told me you were coughing earlier.'

Josh tried to look like someone who might be sickening for 'flu.

'Off you go then home. Are you sure you don't want your mum to come and get you?'

'No, I'll be fine, honest. I only live just up the road.'

'I know where you live, silly,' said Mrs Jackson. People like her always knew everything.

Josh stepped out into the corridor and made his way towards his classroom, feeling very strange and dislocated by the empty echoing sound, by being thrown back into regular school when it had already finished and most people had left. He was himself so empty he thought he might float away, and began to walk with an extra firmness, as if to anchor himself to the ground. Sleeping during the day had always left him confused. It took a while to readjust to your proper time and place. Thank goodness he would be soon be home. He couldn't wait. He'd mentioned to his mother that morning that it would probably be a good idea if Grandma Helen cleaned his and Molly's bedrooms first, so that when they got back from school they could go upstairs out of her way, and Mum had nodded in agreement, though secretly Josh thought it unlikely that if Grandma Helen decided to clean their house from the bottom up, Mum would have much say in the matter.

'Oh, there you are,' said William Beresford. 'I wondered if you'd gone home.'

'Sick Bay,' Josh said, looking round the classroom. Everyone else had left. 'Did I miss anything?'

'Not really. We had a quiz.'

'How much did you win by?'

'Fourteen points,' said William. 'I thought for a while about stopping answering, but then I thought oh well, who cares? Hey – did your bag just move?'

'Just – things shifting inside,' Josh said, moving the bag out of William's view.

'So I thought I'd try and hang around here until the Mob had left. They weren't looking too happy.'

'Shane and Dylan and them?'

William nodded. 'I don't think they've beaten anyone up for a while. They looked *hungry*.'

Josh didn't know what to say. On the one hand it was pretty dumb to win a quiz by fourteen points if you valued your skin. On the other hand it was brave – maybe foolishly brave, but brave nonetheless – to *know* that, and to do it anyway. Josh certainly wouldn't have had the nerve.

'Oh well,' he said. 'I have to go and get my sister from the Infants. It's late. *Very* late,' he added, glancing up at the clock. 'You coming?'

'OK. Let's use the side gate. I wouldn't put it past them to have an ambush waiting at the front. Are you *sure* there isn't something moving in your bag?'

''Course not,' Josh said hurriedly, picking his bag up and swinging it over his arm. Don't be sick, Sabine, he prayed silently. Think of it as a roller coaster ride. We'll be home soon.

They pushed open the side door and walked straight into the ambush.

'Well, well, well,' said Shane Walters. 'It's little Squash and his new best friend Wilma sneaking out holding hands. Stayed behind for a cuddle, did we? A cuddle in the Games Room?'

'Oooh, Wilma, let's play chess!' trilled Dylan Brasher in a squeaky falsetto. 'Show me how the queen moves, Wilma.'

Josh closed his eyes and just kept on walking straight ahead, but Shane Walters grabbed his arm and twisted it.

'Where d'you think you're going? It's rude to walk off without stopping to say hello. Didn't anyone teach you any manners, little Squash? Would you like us to teach you some manners?'

'You two are such a cliché,' said William Beresford, sounding bored.

Dylan Brasher stepped forward. 'What did you say?'

'You heard what I said. It's not my fault if you didn't understand it. Maybe if you paid attention in class you might know something, but since all you do is gaze into each other's eyes all day long it's not surprising you've both turned out to be cretins.'

Any hopes Josh had been entertaining of escaping from this encounter undamaged rapidly disappeared. Shane tightened his grip on Josh's arm, twisting it up roughly behind his back. At the same moment, Dylan punched William in the stomach, sending him gasping back against the wall that separated the Infants school from the Juniors.

William was obviously in considerable pain but he wasn't giving up. 'Last time you broke my glasses the bill went straight to your parents and I know for a fact you're neither of you getting any pocket money till it's paid off. Break these and exactly the same thing will happen. I'm just warning you.'

Dylan Brasher snatched William's little round glasses and hurled them against the wall, from where they fell to the ground with a shattering, splintering sound.

It was as if William had been trying to provoke him. And suddenly Josh thought he understood. If they could get Dylan and Shane so furious that they crossed the bad behaviour barrier to the point of no return, maybe they would, finally, be excluded, and the rest of the class could enjoy their last term in peace. It was, in its way, a brilliant plan, the only downside being the likelihood that Josh and William would be spending most of that term in hospital.

Josh was terribly afraid of pain. Already his arm was bent back behind him at such an unnatural angle that he was frightened that if he moved even a millimetre it might snap. Perhaps if he'd been his normal self that would have been enough to frighten him into silence. But Josh wasn't his normal self, not by any means. Hunger and stress and abnormal sleep patterns had left him feeling like someone else altogether. And so he said, calmly:

'You've got a nerve pretending other people go round holding hands when everyone knows you do it yourselves. Under the desk and on the bus. You always sit together and we all know why. The whole school knows. Shanie and Dilly, we call you. Smoochy Shanie and Dilly Dolly Dreamboat, the hottest couple in Year Six . . . ' And then his whole arm exploded into a red-hot pain so agonising that he couldn't even see, he was literally blinded by it, and he screamed and screamed at the top of his voice. The last thing he saw was William's pale face, shocked, astonished but filled with respect and admiration. Then, for a few moments, he knew nothing.

When he opened his eyes again it was to the sight of a small girl racing up like a tornado, arms and legs whirling. Molly, he thought, dully. Molly would have been waiting just the other side of the wall, and she'd heard and come rushing over, and now they were going to hurt his sister.

Molly charged up to Shane Walters and aimed a kick at his groin. Even through the pain and fear Josh felt a jolt of admiration. Molly was such a fine girl! But Shane dodged easily, pulling Josh forward so he took the full impact, which knocked him to the floor. Shane laughed and caught hold of Molly, trapping her arms with one huge fist, pinning her in front of him, squirming, furious, shrieking but quite unable to move.

'Well well. Look what we've got here! Squash's baby sister! Come to save him!'

Blood was soaking through Josh's trousers where his left knee had scraped cruelly across the concrete as he fell, but he didn't even register the pain. What had he done? He had dragged his little sister into this, just because he was too much of a coward to cope without screaming. He could never, ever forgive himself. He began to concentrate with every atom of his being on gathering his strength for a full-scale attack on Shane Walters. If he launched himself full-tilt, Shane would have to let Molly go. He would probably kill Josh, but that didn't matter. He . . .

'That bag just moved,' said Dylan Brasher.

'Huh?'

'Over there.' Dylan, who had William trapped in an

armlock up against the dividing wall, nodded towards Josh's bag. Everyone turned their head to look. The bag rattled, and shifted a few inches to the left.

'There's something alive in there!' Dylan said.

Shane looked at Dylan, and at the bag, and then at Josh, assessing the situation.

'Go and open that bag!' he barked at Josh. Neither he nor Dylan could afford to let go of their captive.

Josh caught a glance of pure terror from Molly.

'No,' he said.

'You don't argue, Squash,' said Shane Walters. 'You do what you're told. Or else just watch what happens to your sister.' He began to twist Molly's arm round behind her, just as he had done with Josh only minutes earlier. Molly let out a strangled cry of pain.

The bag wobbled to the left and then to the right.

Josh stood up. 'Let her go,' he said to Shane. 'I said *let her go*!' There was a brief silence, and then Shane loosened his grip. He still had hold of Molly but he wasn't hurting her any more. The bag had changed things. The balance of power had, microscopically, shifted.

'Don't worry,' Josh mouthed to Molly, who was staring at him, mouth open, unable to speak. He stepped over to his bag and undid the fastening. He could feel the force of four pairs of eyes burning on his back. He pulled out the ice cream tub, and snapped off the lid.

'No!' shrieked Molly, just as Josh put his hand inside and lifted out a small, wide-awake dragon.

For a few moments it was as if the world had stopped.

The five of them, and Sabine, stood there frozen in time, as Sabine looked at them and they looked back at her.

Molly was the first to move, lunging forward in an attempt to wriggle out of Shane Walters' grip. Shane grabbed her roughly by the shoulder. Molly lifted up her foot and kicked backwards as hard as she could, hitting Shane *crack!* right on the shinbone. With a howl of agony, Shane yanked Molly back close against him and slapped her hard on the cheek.

There was a low rumbling, like a distant generator being switched on and revving up for action, followed by a noise that built up from a faint whine to an ear-splitting screech. Smoke began to wisp out of the dragon's nostrils, and with a sudden roar she launched herself into the air, circled three or four times to get her bearings, aimed herself at Shane Walters head and dive bombed, blasting out jets of pure red-hot flame.

Shane Walters let out a scream of shock and pain, and the air crackled with the unmistakable smell of singed hair. Sabine looped the loop and zoomed back down, this time crashing smack into Shane's forehead. Shane staggered back, yelping in terror and covering his face with his hands, but Sabine merely directed her next attack from behind, the two jets of flame burning a pair of blackened tracks through the hair on the back of Shane's head like fire through a cornfield.

It was at that precise moment that Mr Bailey came running round the corner.

22

They were all taken straight to the headmistress's room, where Mrs Phillips, the head, phoned their parents. Mrs Jackson took a still whimpering Molly away to dab something on her cheek, which was pink and swollen from where Shane had hit her. Shane was clearly the more severely injured of the two of them, but nobody seemed terribly concerned about that.

Josh's mother was the first to arrive, closely followed by William Beresford's father, who looked at William's shattered glasses and then at Molly's cheek, and turned white hot with fury.

Nobody was able to locate Dylan Brasher's parents, but Shane Walters' mother made quite a spectacular entrance. She could be heard shouting and cursing in other parts of the building long before she burst into Mrs Phillips' room, smoking a cigarette.

'I'm afraid I'm going to have to ask you to put that out,' Mrs Phillips said in tones of pure ice, and, 'Ask away,' said Shane Walters' mother, dragging a deep lungful and staring back defiantly. Shane Walters' mother looked nothing like any other mother Josh had ever seen. She had the face of a prize fighter that's been knocked about more than somewhat, an enormous flabby bosom far too much of which was visible above a low-cut shiny top, and she absolutely stank of cigarettes and stale sweat.

Mr Bailey opened a window.

'Who's done this to Shane?' bellowed his mother. 'Shane? What happened? Speak up! I can't hear you! You dumb as well as thick?'

Shane, slumped in misery, muttered something inaudible. It took three repetitions and an awful lot of yelling by his mother before anyone was able to make out the words, which were, astoundingly, that Josh Harper had a dragon and he'd set it on him.

His mother put her hands on her hips and hissed. The rest of the grown-ups exchanged glances of sheer bewilderment. None of the children said a word.

Mrs Phillips scratched her head. She had seen many things during her thirty years in the front line of the education system, and heard an extraordinary variety of lies, fictions and excuses, but never before had anybody offered up a dragon for her entertainment. Now she had heard everything. Nothing could possibly ever top this one. Perhaps it was time to retire and write her memoirs.

'Shane has clearly been burned by something,' she said, 'and we need to find out what.'

'Him!' said Dylan Brasher, jabbing a finger in Josh's direction.

'With a dragon, would you say?' Mrs Phillips asked curiously. Dylan opened his mouth, glanced round the room at the expressions on the faces of all the adults present, and closed it again.

They were each made to give their own account of the incident. Mrs Jackson had no real reason to be there after returning Molly from Sick Bay, but she knew a good story when she heard one and had lingered, half-hidden behind Mr Bailey, to enjoy the fun. Now she stepped forward and bore witness to the fact that Josh, far from being in a mood to ambush his fellow pupils with dragons or flamethrowers or anything of the kind, had in fact been very poorly all day, bless him.

Josh and William and Molly, who was still trembling but spoke up firmly just the same, all told stories which tallied perfectly in every detail, though somehow none of them was able to throw any light on the mystery of what had caused the scorching to Shane Walters' head. Molly had been facing the wrong way. Josh had been knocked to the floor. And William explained that after he'd lost his glasses he couldn't see anything at all.

Mr Bailey took Josh aside and searched him and his belongings. Molly gave a gasp of horror, but Josh sent her another 'Don't worry' look, and she kept silent, though biting her lip with tension throughout the search.

Nothing was found on Josh or in his bag that could possibly be used to generate fire.

William was searched as well, although both Shane and Dylan had pointed Josh out repeatedly as the culprit. No one suggested searching Molly, but she insisted on being searched anyway. Molly, a tiny frail wounded figure amidst all these boys four years her senior, had emerged as something of a heroine, and nobody was in a mood to deny her anything.

Nothing was found.

It was really very unfortunate for Shane and Dylan that the search of Dylan's bag turned up a crumpled packet of cigarettes and a lighter. This discovery didn't precisely account for the bruising on Shane's forehead, but nonetheless the case against Josh collapsed on the spot. Shane and his mother were despatched, with advice that she might want to take him to the hospital for someone to take a look at his head, though it didn't sound to Josh as if anybody greatly cared either way.

Josh's mother and William's father were kept behind for a private talk with Mrs Phillips.

Molly said: 'Josh. Sabine's been in your bag all the time. I saw her jump back in. I *saw*!'

Josh said, 'I know.'

Molly wrinkled her brow and said: 'Then why didn't Mr Bailey find her? Was he pretending?'

'Molly – I'll explain later, OK? I'll tell you absolutely everything when we're back at home with Sabine safe upstairs.'

'You promise?'

'I promise.'

William Beresford came up behind them. Josh gave a guilty start.

'I don't think Shane and Dylan will be back, this time,' he said.

Josh nodded. 'You – you did the right thing,' he said awkwardly. 'You were really brave.'

'You weren't so bad yourself,' said William. 'And as for you, Molly – well. I haven't got a sister. But if I did then I'd want one *exactly* like you.'

There was a brief moment while Molly took this in, and then her face lit up in a radiant smile.

'And now,' said William Beresford. 'What about this dragon?'

Josh and Molly exchanged glances.

'Dragon?' Josh said faintly.

'Josh. I might be short-sighted. I'm not *blind.*'

Josh looked at Molly. Could they trust him?

Molly gave a nod.

And then they heard, behind them, the sound of Mrs Phillips' door opening and a conversation spilling out into the corridor.

'OK,' said Josh. 'But there's no time now. I'll tell you tomorrow. It's a long, long story.'

It was some hours before Josh and Molly got the chance to talk in private, because their father, who arrived home seconds after they did, decided to scoop everyone up and drive them straight out for a slap-up meal. It was a squash in the car, with Grandma Helen there as well, but Molly sat on Mum's lap in the back with Josh squeezed in the middle, and somehow they managed. Luke lay quiet and watchful in his car seat. Several times during the journey Josh turned his head to find his baby brother looking at him intently. 'Boo!' Josh said softly. He crossed his eyes, stuck his thumbs in his ears and waggled his fingers. But Luke was after all the Infant Staring Champion of Britain, and nothing could deflect his solemn gaze.

Mum was bursting to tell the whole story, and Josh and Molly were more than happy to leave her to it.

Dad nearly exploded when he heard about Shane Walters hitting Molly.

‘A boy of Josh’s age? Hit my daughter in the face?’ His fist clenched with rage. ‘Just as well I wasn’t there. I’d have been sorely tempted to beat him to a pulp.’

‘I nearly flattened him myself,’ said Mum. ‘Even Mr Beresford, this boy William’s father, he told me he could barely keep his hands off the little brat. And it wasn’t even his kid he hit! But then the brat’s mother arrived, and if she’d started flattening people there’d have been nobody left standing.’

Grandma Helen gave a little gasp. She was in an unusually benign mood, having just spent an entire day rearranging somebody else’s house to her own satisfaction, but the vision of a headmistress’s office strewn with flattened bodies, three of them her own direct descendants, was more than she could take.

‘And how have these boys been punished?’ she asked sharply.

‘Thrown out!’ said Mum with glee. ‘Banished. Expelled. Excluded.’

‘Really?’ Josh looked up. ‘Really and truly? Did Mrs Phillips tell you that?’

‘She did.’

‘Wow.’ So it had worked.

The waitress arrived bearing platters piled high with fried chicken and chips. Josh was so empty that his insides had been making rumbling grumbling noises for the past hour. He’d grabbed a handful of biscuits during the few minutes they’d been at home, but they might as well have been air for all the difference they’d made to his hunger.

‘Tuck in, Helen!’ said Dad, tipping a generous portion

onto Grandma Helen's plate. Grandma Helen, who normally went to considerable lengths to protect her trim waistline, gave another little gasp.

'I really don't think...'

'Nonsense! You must have burned off thousands of calories doing that wonderful job on our house today. Eat up, or you'll faint dead away.' Molly and Josh exchanged startled glances. You couldn't say 'Nonsense!' to Grandma Helen. You simply couldn't. A thunderbolt would tear the sky apart and strike you dead. But Grandma Helen came over all flustered, and said: 'Well, maybe just a little...' and before you could say 'finger-licking good' she was devouring her chicken with the rest of them.

'Is everything all right?' asked the waitress, who had been lingering to admire Luke. There were general satisfied murmurings and grunts. 'Such a lovely baby you've got!' Luke blew a milky bubble and made a little cooing noise. The waitress swooned. 'We get a lot of babies in here that just start crying when the food arrives. I think it's because they can smell the chicken and they think, oh my God, like wow, let me at it! And then they don't get any so they start to scream. But your baby is so good!' There was a silence as the Harpers considered this. 'Enjoy your meal!' said the waitress, departing with a final adoring glance at Luke.

'I completely forgot to tell you,' said Mum. 'What with all that's been going on.'

'Tell me what?' Dad asked. 'More chips, anyone? Here you go, Helen. Tuck in!' Grandma Helen went slightly pink but she raised no objections.

'Luke's better! He didn't cry once today. All day! Well, only for a few minutes when his nappy needed changing. Apart from that he's been perfectly all right! I couldn't believe it. I'm so used to him crying all the time we're at home, I kept panicking in case he was unconscious or something. But he was just sleeping peacefully.'

'All day? Just like that?'

'Just like that. He's over it.'

'Can that be true?'

'Wendy said one day it would just stop,' Mum said.

Dad laid his knife and fork down. 'Today's becoming more than I can take in. Josh is ill all day, and then he and Molly get into a fight with the school bullies who accuse them of summoning a dragon. Or did I dream that bit?'

'A dragon,' said Mum.

'And meanwhile Luke, who's cried non-stop for the last month, is suddenly miraculously recovered.'

'And you've got a nice clean house for once!' said Grandma Helen.

'All in one day!' Dad said.

Put like this, it did sound a bit much. Josh knew that every one of these things was connected to the others. But it would have been totally impossible ever to explain this to Mum and Dad. They'd have to spend the rest of their lives thinking that it had all happened at once, entirely by coincidence.

'Does anybody mind if I have the last piece of chicken?' asked Grandma Helen.

23

'I've worked it out,' said Molly. 'I was thinking about it all through dinner.'

She had certainly been unusually quiet, though Josh had put that down to shock after her ordeal. Her cheek was still pink and swollen where Shane had hit her.

'Grown-ups can't see Sabine, can they? They can't see her and they can't hear her. None of them can. Remember when Dad came into my room and he didn't even notice her? I told you then he couldn't see her. You wouldn't believe me.' Josh pulled a face. It was true. She had said it and he hadn't believed her. 'But this time you knew, didn't you?' Molly went on. 'You knew even before you got searched. That's why you weren't worried.'

'I think I've known for some time,' Josh said, stretching out a hand to stroke the dragon, who was curled up on Molly's lap, dozing. Josh had expected her to start rushing round like a mad thing, after being cooped up all day, not to mention the excitement of her first free flight and a major scorching. He'd had to leave her in the back garden, still in the ice cream tub in his bag, while they'd been out scoffing chicken and chips. It seemed so cruel, especially when Sabine had been the true heroine of the day. She deserved fuss and treats, not more hours of incarceration. But what choice had he had? It was too risky to put her back in the doll's house. They might have returned home to find the house on fire, which even on such an eventful day as this would be one event too many.

But when she finally got her freedom, Sabine had simply staggered over and curled up on Molly's lap. Probably two doses of sleeping mixture in one day had been more than was good for her system. She was hung over.

'It happens like that with grown-ups sometimes,' Josh said. 'They just can't do things. Like with foreign languages. They can learn the language but they can never ever learn to speak it without an accent. Don't you remember Claudio? He and his sister could speak English properly but his parents sounded totally Italian. You get to a certain age and that's it. You're finished. Your brain just can't do it any more.' Josh's voice trailed away as he realised he was rambling. Now that the dreaded moment was so close, was he trying to engineer a delay?

Molly had no idea that there was a dreaded moment looming. 'Well, that's *good*. Why are you looking so miserable? It means we never have to worry about anybody finding her.' She rubbed Sabine's ear, and the dragon made a low, throaty, purring sound.

'Oh, Molly.' It seemed that Molly's thinking had gone no further.

'Oh Molly what?'

'It's more than that. Look. Think about it. Grown-ups can't see her at all. I can see her and hear her but I can't understand her. But you can. You've always known what she's saying. And you can see the air shaking around her. You told me that, once.'

'So?'

Still she didn't get it. 'So the younger people are, the more she affects them. The more they can see and hear and sense.'

'So?'

'So *imagine what it must be like for Luke*! Molly – ever since Sabine arrived here Luke's never stopped screaming. Listen, now.' From downstairs came the familiar sound of their brother wailing. 'He's only a couple of months old. I don't know what it's like for him but it must be terrible. Maybe it's a deafening noise that goes on the whole time. Maybe it's like a high-pitched scream to him. Maybe it's like fingernails down a blackboard. Molly, they use non-stop noise to torture people. It's unbearable. Maybe she makes vibrations that he can feel. And it's not only Luke. Remember when that other baby was here? She started screaming the moment she got inside the house as well.'

'She was a stupid baby,' Molly said mutinously.

'Well, she *was* a stupid baby. But that doesn't mean it's not true. Whenever Luke gets taken out of the house he stops crying. Today when we had Sabine with us at school he didn't cry at all.'

Molly began to slither backwards on the carpet, Sabine still snoozing on her lap, putting distance between them and Josh. She knew what was coming next.

Josh swallowed.

'Molly. We're not going to be able to keep her. It's not just that she breathes fire. She's making our brother ill.' Please understand, he prayed silently. This was tough enough, without having to battle against Molly!

'So you want to throw her out to be eaten by cats? Because you said that's what would happen. Well, I won't let you. I won't!' Molly's eyes blazed. Josh was reminded of the little ball of fury that had come charging into the playground to defend him, just a few hours earlier.

'Of course I'm not going to do that!'

'Then what do you want to do?'

'There's an adoption centre. We're going to have to put her up for adoption.'

'What? Where?'

'On Technopolis.'

'Adopted on the computer?'

'Molly, it's the best thing.'

'Would she – would she still be – real?'

Josh wasn't going to lie to her. 'Molly, I don't think she'd be real in the way she is now. Maybe that happened because we got that account number with all the sixes. But she'd be real like all the other Technomon are.' Please, please, don't ask me what that means, he thought.

Molly didn't ask that. Molly had always had firmer ideas about reality than Josh had himself. 'But would she be happy?' was what she asked.

'All the Technomon are happy! You only have to look! It's cuter than Disneyland. Nothing bad ever happens. They never die. The worst that could ever happen to Sabine would be she might get scale rot, and then her owner would just go to Morgana's Apothecary and buy a pot of anti-fungal cream, and ten minutes later she'd be cured and running around with her friends. And that's another thing. Friends. Flagondra are one of the most sociable types of Technomon. It said that right at the start when I was choosing what type to have. She needs more company, Molly. All she's got is us and we're at school all day. Even if she wasn't upsetting Luke, it wouldn't be right for us to keep her. It would be selfish.' Molly chewed the side of her finger, and said nothing. 'She needs to be with her own kind,' Josh added. He was starting to sound like the last ten minutes of a particularly soppy film, he knew. He could almost hear the sad music start to play, as the kid prepares itself to say goodbye forever to the best friend it's ever had in the world. It seemed that Josh had seen dozens of films that ended that way, and over the last year or two he'd started to snigger at them for being so mushy and so predictable, and at Molly for enjoying them. Now he knew what it felt like. Perhaps this was his punishment for being so mean. He'd never snigger again.

Molly said: 'Tell me how this adoption thing works.'

'Well – you put your Technomon in the Adoption Centre, and a new owner can pick her out instead of hatching an egg. I had a look when I started. They were all Level 1 Technomon, just babies. They couldn't do anything. Sabine's Level 9 and she's got massive stats and all kinds of skills. She'll get snapped up just like that. You don't need to worry.'

Molly looked appalled. 'You'd let her be adopted by a stranger? How do you know they'd be good to her? It might be someone horrible. How d'you know they'd feed her properly and give her toys?'

'Well – we just have to trust that won't happen.' It sounded pretty feeble. What if Sabine was grabbed by some spoiled kid who got bored with her two days later when his parents bought him a puppy?

'I won't let you do it,' said Molly, and her eyes flashed dangerously once more. She cupped her hands around the dragon as if to protect her from Josh.

Stalemate. Josh knew he couldn't force her to give Sabine up. He wasn't sure he even wanted to. Had he really planned to pass her over to a total stranger?

And then, suddenly, he knew what to do.

'Minerva,' he said.

'Minerva?'

'I'll ask Minerva to adopt her. Minerva's been so good to us whenever we've been in trouble. Surely you trust her? You have to, Molly. There's no other way.'

Molly heaved a deep sigh, but she didn't say no. 'How do you know that Minerva would get there first? You said Sabine would get snapped up.'

'We wouldn't need to use the Adoption Centre. There's an option to send a Technomon directly to another owner. I've seen it. Maybe people swap them.'

Molly thought for a while, and then, in a very small voice, she said: 'OK.'

'I'll go and write to her now,' said Josh. This was going to be the hardest thing he'd ever done in his life, and he was scared that if he didn't do it straightaway he'd lose his nerve.

Molly said nothing.

Josh tiptoed downstairs and sat at the computer. Over the sound of Luke's crying, he could hear his mother's voice: 'But he was fine all day while my mother was here! It must be something I'm doing wrong!'

This had all gone on much, much too long.

To: *Minerva*
From: *Shadow Demon*
We aren't going to be able to take proper care of our Flagondra any more. We are very sad about it.
(He felt it was important that Minerva know this.)
Would you like to have her? She's very friendly and affectionate, and is Level 9 with agility 38, strength 29 and speed 25. She can juggle and is excellent at football, basketball shooting and skateboarding. We want her to have a good home. Her name is Sabine.

He read this through twice, and then pressed **Send**. It was done.

'Sabine's woken up,' Molly said. 'Did you do it?'

Josh nodded. Sabine was playing catch with Molly. He couldn't bear to look either of them in the eye. 'I ordered her a snowball,' he said.

'Frosted double choc chip fudge?'

'Of course. And a smoothie.'

'What flavour?'

'Honeyblossom nectar.'

'Good.'

'They're just arriving now,' Josh said, seeing a small

whirlwind in the air over the mousemat. He fetched the drink and the snowball – the last ever snowball? – and handed them over to Molly.

There was no reason why it should be the last snowball. 'We'll still have the account, you know,' he said.

'Huh?'

'The account with owner number 6,666,666. Even if we don't have an actual Technomon, we can still order things from the shops. Tiny little miniature food and toys and furniture and weapons and plants. That'll be fun, won't it, Molly? You can use them in all your games. It's not as if it's all over.' Josh clung to this thought. Their time with Sabine had been extraordinary, and it would be hard to go back to being just regular kids again. It was a comfort to think that they'd still have some access to the magic.

But Molly just gave him a dark look. 'What use is any of that without Sabine? What's the use of a gourmet snowball without anyone to feed it to?'

'But the toys,' Josh said, his voice faltering. 'You can use those. With your dolls. And we can buy a lot of plants and make a miniature garden. Wouldn't that be fun?'

Molly gave him a quelling look, and he said no more. Sabine was tucking into her gourmet snowball with relish. Her last meal with us, thought Josh, and she doesn't even know.

Suddenly Molly said: 'How is Minerva going to collect her?'

'I suppose she'll go back the way she came,' Josh said. He had thought about this already.

Molly frowned. 'She came in an egg.'

'I mean – the mousemat will take her. I expect it works both ways.'

'Oh.'

There was a long, awkward silence, broken only by a sneeze from Sabine.

'Owww!' yelped Molly. 'It burned me!' Tiny glowing fragments had landed on her arm like sparks from red-hot coals. She slapped them away. One was still glowing as it hit the carpet. Josh stamped on it.

'Go and see if Minerva's answered yet,' Molly said. 'She always did answer right away before.'

'OK.'

Josh went down to the computer, to be told: 'You have Technomessages awaiting!'

To: *Shadow Demon*
From: *Minerva*
Well! As it happens my current brood includes a young male Flagondra called Gabriel who is dying for a playmate. Send Sabine along. She sounds quite remarkable.

That was it, then. Josh's stomach lurched. It was really going to happen.

He wrote a reply, thanking Minerva, and listing all Sabine's favourite foods and activities. He added 'Please let us know if she has arrived safely and settled down happily with you' and then deleted it, because if he said that and then no message came, it would be devastating. Whereas if they hadn't asked, and no message came, there would be no reason to imagine Sabine was anything other than fine.

He pressed **Send** and then selected the option to **Send Technomon to New Owner**. He typed in Minerva's name, and Sabine's. That was all. One click and she would be gone. He hovered with the mouse over the **Send Technomon** button for some seconds. This was really the point of no return. Please, please, let there not be another window asking him **Are you quite sure**?

He pressed **Send Technomon**. There were no more windows. A message popped up saying: 'Technomon Sabine (Flagondra) sent from Shadow Demon to Minerva.'

And that was it.

'Put her on the mousemat,' he said to Molly.

'You're not going to say goodbye?'

Josh hadn't been sure he could cope with saying goodbye, but if Molly was being strong then he must find a way to be strong too. He took the dragon in his hands. 'Hey, Sabine,' he whispered. 'You've been brilliant. You've been the best thing that ever happened to me in my entire life.' Sabine beamed up at him, wrinkling her nose. 'No, don't sneeze! Don't . . . ! ' But it was too late. Sabine made a noise like 'sploooof!' and sparks flew out through her nostrils, catching Josh on the back of his hand.

'Ow!'

'Now she's left us both some burn marks to remember her by,' Molly said. 'It stops hurting in a few seconds.'

Josh carried Sabine over and sat her firmly on the middle of the mousemat.

'Wait! What about her toys? She can't go without them! She'll be so lonely!'

'Molly, we can't send all her toys with her. Minerva will buy her toys. I know she will. I sent her a list of what she likes.'

'Well, she can't buy her a new Teddy Sheringham. He's all chewed and nibbled and he smells of her.'

'Find him then, quick. We don't have much time!'

Teddy Sheringham was still in the ice cream tub. Molly fished him out and pressed him into Sabine's hand. They looked so lost and alone together, the dragon and the tiny turquoise bear, waiting on the mousemat. And then the air began to swirl and to shimmer, much more strongly than ever before, and there was a deep roaring noise, and a silver glow of such a high intensity that Josh couldn't look at it without hurting his eyes. And when he looked back, the mousemat was empty.

It was over.

Downstairs, silence filled the house as Luke stopped crying.

24

'You two look completely wiped out,' said Mum, who was stirring something on the stove. 'Would you like some hot chocolate?'

Josh and Molly nodded. They hadn't been able to stand it upstairs, surrounded by all Sabine's things and no Sabine. Never had a room felt so empty.

'Strictly speaking, it's Molly's bedtime,' Mum said. Josh looked at the clock. It was only ten past eight. How was that possible? It felt like midnight. So much had happened in one day. 'But I don't think we're going to bother much about bedtimes tonight.' Nobody had actually noticed what time they'd been going to bed for weeks. Maybe all that was about to change.

'How's Luke?' asked Josh. His brother was sitting in his father's lap, wide awake and beady-eyed.

'Well, he seems to be fine *now*,' said Dad. 'He was screeching the place down for ages after we got home. As usual. And then he suddenly stopped. He was clenched up and pink and furious, and then for some reason he completely relaxed, drank a bottle of milk and started blowing bubbles. Just like that. I've never known anything like it.'

'I think he's going to be all right now,' Josh said quietly. Luke made a noise that sounded like 'bluh'.

The telephone rang. For a crazy moment Josh thought

it must be Sabine, calling to let them know she'd arrived safely. Nobody moved. Two rings, and the phone stopped.

'Wrong number,' said Dad.

'That reminds me!' said Mum, taking the pan of milk off the stove and pouring it into the mugs she had lined up in a row. 'Teresa di Carlo phoned, Josh. There's been so much going on since then, I forgot all about it.'

'Me? *Who*?'

'Claudio's mother!'

'Oh!' This was the very last thing Josh had been expecting. 'Why? Is something wrong with Claudio?'

'Claudio's fine. They were more worried that something was wrong with you. Claudio's sent you three or four e-mails recently, and you haven't answered any of them. They wondered if you'd changed your e-mail address, or if you'd been ill.'

Josh simply hadn't thought to check his e-mail for weeks. He hadn't even thought about Claudio. Sabine had taken up every second of his energy.

'I'll have a look tomorrow,' he said.

'You'll be doing more than that,' said his mother. 'I said you'd call them back.'

'On the phone? To *Italy*? Why?'

'Because you're invited to go and stay for a week of the Easter holidays!'

'Oh!'

'What a marvellous opportunity,' said Josh's father. 'You do want to go, don't you, Josh? You're not looking exactly thrilled.'

'Just taking it in,' said Josh, whose first thought had

been: 'But I can't. I can't leave Molly to look after Sabine on her own.' He'd become so used to thinking like that. And now – well, now he was free again. He had loved Sabine. Of course he had. But – a trip to Italy? To stay with Claudio?

'Would I be going on an aeroplane?' he asked. 'On my own?'

'You certainly would,' said his father. 'It'll be a brilliant adventure.'

'Rome will be so much warmer than here,' said his mother. 'I'm jealous!'

'And we'll expect you to come back speaking fluent Italian!' said his father.

Josh's face broke into a smile. He couldn't help it. It was the biggest treat he'd ever had in his life. He'd never really believed he would see Claudio again. And Easter was only ten days away! He almost wished it were further, so he'd have more time to look forward to it.

Then he remembered Molly, who was sitting very silent and still, and his spirits sank. If only there could have been a treat for Molly too. Now she'd not only lost Sabine, but she'd be on her own with Mum and Luke for a great chunk of the Easter holidays as well. Molly had always been pretty good at amusing herself, but just the same . . .

His father caught his sideways glance at his sister.

'Sorry we don't have a surprise for you too, Moll,' he said. 'But I'm taking a week off work, and we'll go out on some trips, just the four of us. We'll have a good time.'

'It's OK,' Molly said. 'I'm glad Josh is going. Really I am.'

Their father looked at her a while longer, and then suddenly said: 'Hey! Whatever happened to those eggs?'

'Eggs?'

'The famous Easter Egg Hunt you invented! All those little coloured eggs in baskets. Now Easter is so close, and Luke seems so much better, don't you think it's time to get it out again and start doing it properly? I've spotted several excellent hiding places.'

'OK,' said Molly.

'What happened to the eggs?' asked Mum.

'I put them up on a very high shelf out of temptation's way,' said Dad. 'Here, someone take Luke and I'll go and fetch them right now.'

Josh held his arms out, and his father passed the baby over. 'Hi there, Luke.' Was it his imagination, or did Luke feel more solid than the last time he'd held him. 'How are you doing?' Luke eyed him serenely, reached out a tiny hand and curled it firmly round Josh's finger. And Josh thought: 'Oh!' For the first time, he felt a connection. This was his *brother*. And he recognised him. And he quite certainly wasn't going to die.

Luke might be only the same size as a newborn baby but his face was older and wiser. He looked as if he'd been around for a long time and seen a great many things.

You're going to be my brother for the rest of my life, Josh thought, looking down into the baby's blue-eyed gaze. You'll never know a world that didn't have me in it. When you're starting school I'll be doing my GCSEs. When you're the age I am now I'll be grown up. Maybe you'll look just like me and it'll be like watching myself through a time machine. And maybe one day I'll be reading to you in bed and I'll put the book down and tell you a story about a little red dragon, which you'll like better than all the books put together, and you'll ask for it again and again.

Luke blinked, blew a bubble, wrinkled his nose and threw up all over him.

25

To: *Shadow Demon*
From: *Minerva*
I thought you'd be happy to know that Sabine has arrived safe and sound. She's eating me out of house and home, and she and Gabriel play ball games together all day long. She's quite a character, isn't she? I knew straightaway that she'd had a very special upbringing.
Yours
Minerva (Owner No: 5,555,555)

26

The shed door opened and a small figure slipped inside. Further progress was difficult. The way was blocked by a rickety wardrobe and a dusty old tea chest, piled high with cardboard boxes. But this apparently impassable obstacle was an illusion. The boxes were empty and could be lifted down to the floor, just an armful of cardboard. And the tea chest, which looked so heavy, was made of paper-thin wood, and was empty too, and it was no trouble at all to push it aside six inches or so, just enough to open up a gap through which a very small person could slide.

The welcoming chorus of squeaks and squawks started up as soon as Molly entered the shed. The birdcage hanging from the ceiling had been cleaned up, and now contained a four-day-old Glostrich, admiring itself in a round mirror, the frame encrusted with sparkly stones. The old kitchen sink had been filled up with clean water, and a small Springray, glowing faintly green and blue, was whooshing from one end to the other like a torpedo. A pair of young Luponio had their home in the gramophone. At the sight of Molly they scampered onto the turntable, their own private roundabout, ready for a ride.

'Hello, boys,' Molly said, setting them off spinning. Squeals of excitement. Molly smiled indulgently. She had initially been a bit disappointed when both her

Luponio eggs hatched into males, but had quickly become much too attached to them to want them changed in any way. She'd expected that all Technomon, whatever their breed, would behave exactly like Sabine, but this was far from the case. The Luponio were more adventurous, more determined and a very great deal more active. The Boboloon was more highly-strung than the other Technomon, and sudden loud noises made it nervous, but Molly could tell already that it was highly intelligent. The Springray, in the way of underwater things everywhere, kept its personality a closely guarded secret. And the Glostrich was a total airhead.

On top of the disused fridge lay the Technomon mousemat, while in a padded basket on the middle shelf of the fridge nestled a pink egg with lime green speckles, due, sometime in the next twenty-four hours, to hatch into a Chipsqueak. Half a dozen newly ordered bottles of infant food were sitting on the mousemat, awaiting Molly's attention.

Molly had needed quite a lot of computer time to get all this set up. It was probably just as well that Josh was away in Italy. It was sad in a way that he wasn't going to be involved, but Molly knew it was for the best. Josh didn't have the right temperament to care for Technomon. He worried too much. Molly never worried about anything. She couldn't see the point.

It was also fortunate that Molly had such a remarkable memory. She hadn't the least idea how that complicated game CipherMaster worked, the one with the coloured jewels that Josh had learned from William

Beresford. But she was brilliant at Memory Match. She could memorise the entire layout and clear the screen without needing to guess even once. She was making a small fortune in Technickels. All her Technomon would have the very finest toys.

And the shed was the perfect place to keep them. Any burglars crafty enough to get past Molly's obstacles would simply see an old fridge, a filing cabinet, a record player and an empty birdcage. And Luke, well out of the way indoors, was thriving, undisturbed by noise or vibrations. In a few years when he was a proper person, Molly might let him in on the secret. By then Josh would be a teenager. Maybe he wouldn't be able to see Technomon any more. Maybe by then he'd have persuaded himself that Sabine had been nothing more than a dream. Probably he'd be happier that way.

The Glostrich made one of its sudden squawks, and the Boboloon, whose name was Mungo, scampered over to Molly, chattering anxiously.

'It can't hurt you, silly,' said Molly, picking up the monkey, who looked up at the birdcage and whimpered. 'Yes, OK. I know you're hungry. I'll feed you all in a minute.' Josh had made it sound as if Molly would some day grow too old to understand what Technomon said, but she didn't believe that for one moment. OK, so maybe you couldn't learn to speak Italian without an accent when you were grown up, but if you'd learned it when you were younger, wouldn't you know it forever? It was Molly's opinion that you would, and that this was just the same thing.

A tiny noise came from the fridge. Molly peered inside, and saw that a faint crack had fractured the pink and green Chipsqueak egg. A tremor of excitement ran through her. Every single egg so far had hatched in her absence. Now, at last, she'd be able to see the miracle for herself. She picked up the Boboloon's bottle of banana milk ready for its afternoon feed, and curled up on the floor to watch.